PENGUIN BOOKS

SUDDENLY

ISABELLE AUTISSIER is the first woman to have sailed around the world solo in competition. She was a navigator until 1999, and is currently the president of the French chapter of the World Wildlife Fund. She has published several stories and novels, and was awarded the Légion d'honneur, Chevalier des Arts et des Lettres for her literary work.

GRETCHEN SCHMID has translated several works from French into English, among them Haitian novelist and poet Lyonel Trouillot's *Kannjawou*. She is also an editor at HarperCollins.

Suddenly

Isabelle Autissier

Translated by Gretchen Schmid

PENGUIN BOOKS

PENGUIN BOOKS

An imprint of Penguin Random House LLC
penguinrandomhouse.com

Originally published in French as *Soudain, seuls*
by Éditions Stock, Paris.

LIBRARY OF CONGRESS CATALOGING-IN-PUBLICATION DATA
Names: Autissier, Isabelle, 1956– author. | Schmid, Gretchen, translator.
Title: Suddenly / Isabelle Autissier ; translated by Gretchen Schmid.
Other titles: Soudain, seuls. English
Description: [New York] : Penguin Books, [2023] |
"Originally published in
French as Soudain, seuls by Éditions Stock, Paris."—Title page verso.
Identifiers: LCCN 2023006926 (print) | LCCN 2023006927 (ebook) |
ISBN 9780143137429 (trade paperback) | ISBN 9780593511459 (ebook)
Subjects: LCGFT: Novels.
Classification: LCC PQ2661.U799 S6813 2023 (print) | LCC PQ2661.U799
(ebook) | DDC 843/.914—dc23/eng/20230213
LC record available at https://lccn.loc.gov/2023006926
LC ebook record available at https://lccn.loc.gov/2023006927

Printed in the United States of America
1st Printing

Set in Walbaum MT Pro
Designed by Sabrina Bowers

Suddenly

PART I

There

THEY SET OUT EARLY. The day promises to be sublime, as days sometimes are in these wild latitudes; the sky is a deep blue, almost liquid, with the clearness particular to the southern Fifties. There isn't so much as a wrinkle on the surface of the water, and the *Jason*, their boat, seems to float weightlessly on a carpet of dark sea. Without any wind, the albatrosses pedal calmly around the hull.

They pull the dinghy high up on the shore and walk around the old whaling station. The rusty sheet metal, gilded by the sun, is a mix of ochers, browns, and reds, giving off a jaunty air. Abandoned by man, the station has been taken over by animals, the same ones that for so long had been hunted, felled, disemboweled, and cooked in the enormous boilers that are now falling into ruin. As they wander from one pile of bricks to the next, they find collapsed sheds containing jumbles of pipes that no longer lead anywhere, in the middle of which groups of cautious penguins, families of fur seals, and elephant seals are lounging. They stay to watch the animals for some time, and it is late in the morning when they begin to go up the valley.

"Three solid hours," Hervé, one of the few people to have ever been here, had told them. On the island, as soon as you get away from the coastal plain, there is no more green. The

world becomes mineral: rocks, cliffs, peaks crowned by glaciers. They walk at a good clip, bursting into laughter when
they see the color of a stone or the purity of a stream as
though they're kids skipping school to go on an adventure.
When they arrive at the first steep slope, before they lose
sight of the sea, they take another break. It's so simple, so
beautiful, almost inexpressible—the bay encircled by blackish drop-offs, the water glinting silver in the light breeze
that's beginning to blow, the old station an orange splotch,
and their good old boat, which seems to be sleeping, its wings
folded under itself like the albatrosses from that morning.
Off the coast, motionless white-blue behemoths gleam in
the light. There is nothing more peaceful than an iceberg in
calm weather. The sky is streaked with enormous stripes—
high, shadowless clouds, fringed with gold by the sun.

They stay for a long time, fascinated, savoring the sight.
Probably a little too long. Louise notices that it is beginning
to get gray in the west and her mountaineering antennae
prick up, on alert.

"Don't you think we should go back? The clouds are coming this way."

Her tone is falsely cheerful, but a hint of unease comes
through.

"Of course not! Come on, you're always worrying about
something. We won't be so hot if there's some cloud cover."

Ludovic tries to keep impatience out of his voice, but
frankly, he's irritated by her anxiety. If he had always listened to her, they wouldn't even be here, alone on this island
at the edge of the world as though they were its king and

queen. They would have never bought their boat or gone on this incredible journey. Sure, the sky is growing dark in the distance, but at worst they will just get wet. This is the price of adventure, it's the whole point—to escape the torpor of the Parisian offices that was threatening to envelop them in comfortable softness, leaving them on the sidelines of their own lives. Their sixties would arrive and they would have nothing but regrets for never having lived, never having struggled, never having discovered anything. He forces himself to speak in a conciliatory tone.

"Hey, it's now or never that we go see that amazing dry lake. Hervé told me that you wouldn't see anything like it anywhere else—a maze of ice on the ground. You remember the incredible photos he showed us. And besides, I'm not lugging around the ice axes and crampons for nothing. It'll be awesome, you'll see, for you especially."

He has touched a nerve. She is the mountaineer. He had chosen the destination with her in mind: a southern but mountainous island with a jumble of peaks, each purer than the last, right in the middle of the Atlantic Ocean, at a latitude of more than fifty degrees south.

IT IS ALREADY two p.m. and the sky is downright dark by the time they reach the last peak. Hervé hadn't lied; the dry lake is astounding, a perfect oval crater more than a kilometer long. It is entirely empty, its sides lined with concentric curves left by the receding water, like the half-moons of giant fingernails. There is no water left at all. A strange siphoning phenomenon had caused the lake to empty underneath a rocky barrier. In the old basin nothing remains but gigantic pieces of ice, some of them several dozens of meters high—a testament to the time when they were all one structure, with a glacier below them. How long had they been there, crammed side by side like a forgotten army? Under the now-gray sky, the monoliths, speckled with old dust, give off an air of poignant melancholy. Louise pleads once again for them to turn around.

"We know where we are, we'll be able to come back. It's not worth getting soaked . . ."

But Ludovic is already hurtling down the slope, whooping with pleasure.

They wander for a bit through the chunks of ice. Close up, the ice seems sinister. The whites and blues, ordinarily dazzling, are stained with dirt. Some of it is slowly melting, tarnishing the surface and giving it the look of a piece of parchment devoured by insects. Nevertheless, Ludovic and Louise are captivated by the ice's gloomy beauty. Sliding their hands over the worn-out cavities and caressing the cold exteriors, they muse that the ice melting before their very eyes existed well before them, well before *Homo sapiens* started to turn the entire planet upside down. They start whispering, as though they're in a cathedral, as though their voices threaten to upset the fragile balance.

The rain beginning to fall interrupts their contemplation.

"Look, this ice isn't in great condition. Hervé may have had fun climbing on it, but honestly, I don't see the point. It would be much better for us to hurry back. The wind is picking up and that might be tough for the dinghy's little motor."

Louise is no longer just grumbling; she has switched to issuing commands. Ludovic knows this tone of voice is not to be questioned. He also knows that she often has good intuition and judgment. All right, they'll turn around.

They climb back up the crater and run down the slope toward the valley. Their jackets are already flapping in the breeze, and their feet are sliding on the damp rocks. The weather has changed rapidly. When they reach the last pass, they notice wordlessly that the bay looks nothing like the peaceful sight they had seen on the way there. An evil spirit has caused its surface to go murky with raging waves. Louise is running and Ludovic is stumbling behind her, grumbling. They arrive at the beach out of breath. The waves are crashing chaotically. In the swell that forms, they can see their boat rocking forcefully at the end of its chain.

"Well, we'll get soaked, and then we'll deserve some nice hot chocolate!" says Ludovic confidently. "Go in front and row right into the wave while I push. As soon as we've passed the breaker zone, I'll start the motor."

They drag the dinghy, looking for a lull in the waves. The freezing water churns around their knees.

"Now! Go! Row, for God's sake, row!"

Ludovic is slipping in the wet sand while Louise struggles with her oar in front of him. A wave breaks, filling the little boat with water, and then another wave catches the boat askew, lifting it up and tipping it upside down as though it were nothing but a piece of straw. They find themselves thrown against each other in a whitish, seething swirl.

"Shit!"

The dinghy is already being swept away by the waves. With one hand, Ludovic catches its rope. Louise massages her shoulder.

"The outboard motor hit me in the back. It hurts."

They are standing next to each other, dripping wet and stupefied by the sudden violence.

"Let's drag the dinghy over to that corner of the beach, where the waves aren't breaking as much."

Resolutely, they haul the tiny boat to a place that seems more promising. But when they get there, it becomes clear that it's not much better. They attempt the maneuver twice more; both times they are thrown back into a whirlpool of foam.

"Stop! We'll never make it and I'm in too much pain."

Louise lets herself collapse on the ground. She holds her arm, grimacing, the tears falling from her eyes invisible thanks to the rain whipping her face. Ludovic kicks the ground angrily, sending a spray of sand into the air. He is overcome with frustration and rage. This fucking place! This fucking island, fucking wind, fucking sea! If they'd been half an hour earlier—an hour, max—they would be drying themselves off in front of the stove and laughing about the whole thing right now. He is furious about his powerlessness and the sense of remorse that is painfully starting to set in.

"Okay, we won't make it. Let's just go find shelter in the station and let this pass. The wind picked up fast—it'll die down soon."

With difficulty they pull the dinghy high up onto the beach, tie it to an ancient gray pole, and start off among the remnants of planks and sheet metal.

Over the past sixty years, the wind has taken its toll on the old whaling station. Some of the buildings have been blown up from the inside, as though by an explosion. Flying rocks have broken the windows and violent winds have taken care of everything else. Other structures are leaning perilously, waiting for the final blow to finish them off. Next to the wooden ramp on which whales were dragged to be dismembered is a shed that catches Louise's and Ludovic's attention. But inside it smells so horrible that they gag. Four elephant seals all lying on top of each other belch noisily at the intrusion.

Annoyed, Louise and Ludovic venture farther into the ruins toward a two-story shack that seems to be in better shape. A waddle of imperturbable penguins crosses their path, and Ludovic is tempted to chase them to make them regret their indifference. The inside of the building is gloomy, dark, and damp. The old floor tiles, metal tables, and decrepit cooking pots reveal that the room they are in must once have functioned as a shared kitchen. The room next door does in fact look like a dining hall. Louise collapses onto a bench, trembling. She's in pain, but most of all she's afraid. She understands a mountain's temperament, knows how to deal with its fits of rage: at worst, you wrap yourself in a bivvy sack, burrow into the snow, and wait. But here she feels lost.

Ludovic mounts the concrete stairs. At the top he finds two vast dormitories, cubicles separated by half partitions that each contain a battered mattress, a small table, and a wide-open wardrobe. Faded photos, a single lace-up boot, and tattered clothing hanging from a nail give the rooms the appearance of having been hastily abandoned by men who were all too happy to escape this hell. In the back, a door hanging half off its hinges leads to a little room with wooden shiplap walls that's furnished much more nicely: probably the bedroom of a supervisor.

"Come on, it's better up here. We can wait in the warmth."

"Warmth" is a generous way of putting it. They sit on the bed, which creaks underneath them. The rain slaps against the loose windowpanes, seeping in; already a pond has formed in a rotting corner of the floor. Greenish light illuminates the streaks of moisture on the whitewashed walls. The only chair is broken, and for some reason Ludovic finds himself wondering why. Only a desk with drawers, much like the kind that teachers used at the turn of the century, appears intact.

"Well, here's our mountain refuge! Let's take a look at your shoulder. And we have to dry ourselves off."

He's making an effort to speak soothingly, to give the impression that this is nothing but an adventure, but his hands are trembling lightly. He helps her undress so that they can dry her sopping-wet clothes. Naked, her thin and muscular body appears fragile. She had always refused to sunbathe when they were in warmer climates. As a result, only her arms, face, and the bottoms of her legs are tanned, making the rest of her complexion appear even paler. Her black bangs are dripping onto her eyes, which are green with flecks of brown. Those eyes were the first thing about her that he had found irresistible, five years earlier. He's overcome by a wave of affection.

He wrings out her clothes and rubs her body with her sweater as fast as he can to warm her up. Her left shoulder has a sizable gash—from the propeller, presumably—and a large blotch that is already turning blue. Shivering, she lets him handle her as though she were a doll. He does the same thing for himself, but soon feels the chill of the soaking-wet clothes that are sticking to his skin. In the summer, even in good weather, it barely gets above sixty degrees here. Right now it must be somewhere around fifty degrees.

"Do we have a lighter?" he asks her.

"In the bag."

Of course she—the alpinist—would never go anywhere without her precious lighter. He also finds two emergency blankets and quickly wraps her up in one.

Rummaging through the kitchen, he unearths some kind of large aluminum roasting pan and pulls some boards down from shelves that are falling to pieces. Taking it all back upstairs, he cuts some small slivers from the boards with his knife and uses them to light a small fire. The room fills quickly with smoke, despite the open door, but it's better than no fire at all.

He forces himself to go outside to investigate the situation.

The wind has intensified, its gusts causing the sea to appear as if it's smoking. A solid forty knots. Not the apocalypse, but still, it will be impossible to get back to the boat. He can see it between the sheets of rain, staying valiantly upright among the waves. The cloudy gray sky has descended so low that the tops of the cliffs are no longer visible, and it is growing dark.

"Looks like we're here for the night," he announces when he returns from outside. "Is there anything left to eat?"

Louise has recovered a bit of energy. She's keeping the fire going, which is comforting even though the old boards are giving off a terrible smell of tar as they burn. They hang their jackets up near the flames and huddle together, chewing on granola bars.

Neither one of them has any desire to talk about the situation. They both know it's dangerous terrain, that to do so would force them to confront each other: Louise, the cautious one, versus Ludovic, the impetuous one. The argument will come later, when this unpleasant episode is in the past. They'll analyze everything that happened. She'll try to prove to him that they had been reckless, and he'll retort that the situation had been unforeseeable; they'll bicker and then they'll make up. It's become almost a ritual by now, a safety valve for their differences. Neither one will admit defeat, but both—convinced of their own rightness—will agree to bury the hatchet. For now, though, they have to stay united and wait this out.

With eyes reddened by the smoke, they dry off, surrounded by a growing cacophony. On the lower level, the wind is roaring through the abandoned rooms, a relentless low modulation punctuated by cries that grow shriller with each gust of wind. At times a brief respite sets in and they can feel their muscles relax in unison. But then the growling starts up again, seemingly even louder than before. Here and there, pieces of metal clang against each other, the sound reverberating. Louise and Ludovic stay silent, each of them engrossed in the gloomy symphony. Fatigue——from the hike, and perhaps more notably, from their emotions——comes crashing over them. Finally, Ludovic unearths a blanket that smells like old dust; the two of them curl up on the little bed and fall asleep immediately.

Ludovic awakens in the night. The sounds have changed. He deduces that the wind has shifted, and that now it is coming from the land. It has gotten even more violent. He can hear its grumbling coming from far up on the mountain, hurtling down to the valley like a drumroll before striking the building, which seems to sway from the blows. He considers the wind's change of direction to be a good sign; the end of the storm is approaching.

Amid the darkness and the warm dampness of their entangled bodies, he experiences, briefly, a sense of calm. True, the two of them are all alone, without any other human being within a radius of thousands of kilometers, amid extreme wind. But on the other hand, they have found shelter, and later they will be able to laugh about the storm. He has the strange impression that each part of his body is autonomous, separate from the rest of it, and he takes stock of each element of this strange situation: the hollowed, battered mattress underneath his back; Louise's slow breathing against his chest; the wind, seeming to come out of nowhere, that brushes against his head. He is tempted to wake her so that he can make love to her, but then remembers her shoulder is hurting. Better to let her sleep. Tomorrow morning, maybe . . .

A little before dawn, the noise suddenly stops. Half-awake, they both realize that the storm has passed, and then fall back asleep, this time completely relaxed.

A ray of sunlight pulls Louise from her lethargy. Until the storm ended, she had been having nightmares. She dreamed that the windows in their apartment in the fifteenth arrondissement had been blasted by a monstrous wave, and that she was drifting on a raft through streets flooded with brown water, surrounded by calls of distress and arms waving desperately from the windows.

"Ludovic, are you asleep? It seems like it's over!"

They shake out their bodies, which have grown stiff. Louise grimaces as she sits up, feeling her injured shoulder at length with her other hand.

"I don't think it's broken, but you'll need to take the helm for a while."

"Okay, princess. Let's go. The hotel isn't exactly the height of luxury, but breakfast will be served on board in fifteen minutes, if Madame will oblige."

They smile at each other, collect their things, and leave the room, which has a lingering odor of cold smoke.

Outside, the sun is shining as brightly as it had the day before.

"This fucking place, huh?"

Still standing on the doorstep, they both experience the same feeling. Something seizes their stomachs in a tight grip; an acridness burns in their throats; they are overcome by an uncontrollable trembling.

The bay is empty.

"The boat . . . That's not possible . . . It's not there . . ."

They're stammering, babbling, blinking their eyes as though it will fix the image in front of them. This must all be a bad dream. They just need to rewind the last few hours and start again, and this time everything will go as planned. Upon leaving the station, they were supposed to see the *Jason* still there, immobile and reassuring, and they would walk down to the shore, bantering with each other. But the reality of the situation persists cruelly. The boat has disappeared.

For a long time they scrutinize the bay, looking for a piece of debris or at least a bit of the mast peeking out from behind a cliff. But there's nothing. Or, more accurately, there's only life going on as usual: gulls pecking frantically at the beach, the hissing of the waves pulling back into the sea. Everything looks normal. The *Jason*—their boat, their home, the means of their liberty—has simply been erased, as though it were an error. But this is simply unacceptable. It can't be.

Reeling, they are unable to exchange a single word. The horrifying consequences of their situation are sinking in. No more home. No more food. No more clothing. No way to leave the island or communicate with anyone. Once they've overcome their denial, it is the absurdity of the situation that overwhelms them. Ludovic has simply never for a second imagined that he could someday be without food, shelter, the essentials of life. Whenever he saw impoverished people on TV, he would fend off his pangs of conscience by convincing himself that those people probably didn't need as much as he did—that they were used to living with less. He would sometimes send off a check to UNICEF, but he never felt particularly concerned.

Louise had often slept outside during her mountaineering trips, sometimes while soaked through from rain and with one eye open to watch for danger. Once, for three days, she had even shared rations meant for one person with three other people due to a supply miscalculation. In the middle of the wilderness, far from anything familiar, she had experienced the inherent fragility of being human. But that had been only a brief episode; nothing fundamental was at stake. With no harm done except for shadows underneath their eyes and some stomach cramps, the four climbing partners eventually made it back down into the valley, where they luxuriated in endless showers and steaks, relishing the thrill of having lived through an adventure. In the end, those types of situations just became good memories to laugh about with each other, although at least they have prepared Louise to face the unexpected. Whether by instinct or by training, she knows how to sort the essential from the superfluous and the dangerous from the disturbing. In order to become a good alpinist, she had to learn to reevaluate a goal based on the present circumstances—to turn back or keep going depending on the state of the group, the weather, and other natural conditions. She is therefore the better equipped of the two to pull them out of their lethargy:

"The dinghy, as long as it's still there! We can use it to go look around. The *Jason* was halfway between the cape and the group of rocks across from it. Maybe it sunk right where it was."

"But we would see the tip of the mast!"

Ludovic is struggling with the facts in a different way. Ordinarily he is optimistic, ready for anything, but now he feels empty. Nothing is of any use.

"It could have lost its mast. There can't be more than seven or eight meters of water—we might find some stuff, maybe food or tools. There's a satellite phone in the emergency dry bag. We have to at least try. Come on, let's go!"

"No, I'm sure that it was dragging anchor. I heard it last night. The wind shifted northwest, and it accelerated as it came down from the mountains. A real katabatic wind, just like in the books."

"I don't give a shit about books!" she screams, tears in her eyes. "What do you want to do? Go back to the hotel?"

She takes off in a fury toward the beach and he follows her. The same thoughts are whirling around in both of their heads. The island is deserted. In fact, it's a nature reserve that they shouldn't have landed on in the first place. But they had both decided to break the rules:

"No one will come by anyway. It'll be a chance to experience real nature. And it will just be a quick stop, only a couple of days, no one will ever find out . . ."

And it's true: no one knows. Their friends and family back home think that they're en route to South Africa. They'll never look for them here. They'll just believe them to be lost at sea. Ludovic has a fleeting vision of his parents waiting next to the telephone in their house in the Parisian suburbs. If he and Louise don't find the boat, then this island will become a prison—a prison with no guard except thousands of kilometers of ocean.

The dinghy is still there, covered in sand and seaweed from the storm. This is a small comfort.

For an hour they row around the area where they had cast anchor. The breeze just barely skims the clear water, which is such a translucent green that they can see scattered rocks down at the bottom and a few dark masses that look like machine parts that were lost or removed from the whaling station. There's no way they wouldn't see a shipwreck.

Discouraged, they return to the beach.

"We didn't use enough chain," Louise says unhappily.

"Yes, we did. Three times the depth, just like we usually do."

"Well, obviously there's nothing 'usual' about this place!"

"Also, the Soltant anchor is the best kind. It's supposed to hold anywhere. It certainly cost us enough."

"Oh, then thanks so much, Monsieur Soltant. Is he the one who's going to come find us? We should have used twice as much chain as usual. If we'd done that we wouldn't be in this situation. And I told you yesterday that we should have turned back earlier. But no, you just wanted to have a good time; you dug your heels in and said everything would be fine, we'd just get a little wet . . ."

Louise's voice is flat, full of icy rage. She is nervously rubbing her shoulder, staring at the sand, her back to Ludovic. If she were to look at him, she knows exactly what she'd see: his helpless, large, wrestler's body, with his arms dangling at his sides and his blue eyes like those of a child whose favorite toy has just been broken. The man who's made for the joy and carefreeness that she loves. The sight would make her burst into tears, and it's not the right time for that.

He doesn't want to respond to her criticism. Ever since they had turned back the day before, he has had the bitter taste of regret in his mouth. But her comments have hurt him. He has to find a solution so that she'll forgive him. Surely he must have a solution.

"Maybe we could use the motor and sail around the bay . . . It could have sunk alongside a cliff."

"You're delusional. And even if we found it, what would we do? I don't know how we'd get it afloat again."

"At least we might be able to dive in, rescue some . . ."

Ludovic doesn't finish his sentence. Louise is crying soundlessly. He draws her against his shoulder. How have they gotten themselves into this absurd situation? It doesn't seem fair that they should be punished like this for a stroll that lasted a little too long. He is thirty-four years old and the idea of death has hardly ever crossed his mind. The deaths of two of his friends—one from a motorcycle accident, one from severe pancreatic cancer—had shaken him, but they

also made him all the more determined to go on this sailing trip. They had to live! Live as much as they could, before
something caught up with them! And now it is a balmy
day during the austral summer, and they are in the midst
of a magnificent landscape, and something has caught up
with them.

The duplicitous sun is making the beads of moisture sparkle like thousands of diamonds. In the distance, the plain is
steaming lightly. Fur seals and elephant seals are lounging
around, yawning happily. He looks around him and thinks
that nothing—not a bird's flight, nor a wave, nor a blade of
grass—will change if they disappear here. The wind will
quickly sweep away their footprints.

LUDOVIC IS A quintessential millennial. He grew up in a house in the suburbs, the only son of parents who were both managers, and was given everything he could ever want, from ski trips in Alpe d'Huez and sailing trips in the Balearic Islands to video games to occupy his precious little head whenever his parents were out late. His blond hair—cut with military precision and styled with gel every morning— accentuates his six-foot, three-inch frame. With his blue eyes and dimpled chin, he stole the hearts of all the girls in middle school and then in high school—easy successes that he fully enjoyed.

His lack of follow-through exasperated his teachers; a common refrain on his report cards was "Doesn't live up to his potential." One way or another, he managed to graduate from business school, where he had spent a lot more time drinking beer and smoking weed than attending lectures. With help from some connections of his father, he found a job as an account manager at Foyd & Partners, an event agency that could not be more French despite its name, which was supposed to sound trendy. He took to this somewhat superficial role well, thanks to a strong aptitude for happiness that drew other people to him like a magnet.

Being with him made people feel good; he made life feel simple, fun, fascinating. Not only did he always see the glass half-full, but his enthusiasm and joie de vivre were contagious without him even having to try. His attitude wasn't a facade, or an affectation; it was merely the result of a life that had been protected and happy. He couldn't remember ever having woken up feeling sad, or even slightly melancholy. Little by little, he had come to recognize that this was an unusual ability, but he didn't take particular pride in it. Giving some of his surplus of joy to the people around him was just his nature, his way of contributing to the world. People said that he was a truly nice person.

Louise, at first sight, seems conventional, almost old-fashioned, with a slender frame, an elongated face, and the quick, often forced smile of someone who is trying not to offend. She is the daughter of shopkeepers from Grenoble who still budget carefully despite their financial security; growing up, she didn't want for anything, either, except perhaps some attention. Her two older brothers were the pride and joy of the family, while she, "the little one," slipped through the cracks. Her thoughts, dreams, and academic and personal achievements were never of much interest to her family.

The way she looks reflects the lack of attention she received. Even she thinks so. Five foot one, dark-haired, and bony, she has long despaired over her nonexistent breasts. She had gone through childhood and adolescence without attracting much notice, but she seemed to be okay with this, as though she were seeking forgiveness for her own existence. People said that she was uncomplicated, although this wasn't true. She graduated from high school, studied law in Lyon, took the civil service entrance exam, and found a position in a tax office in Paris's fifteenth arrondissement. During all this time she continued to suffer from a sort of transparency.

As a little girl, she had taken refuge in reading, devouring books by Jules Verne, Émile Zola, and anything else she could find at the library. Thanks to these, she spent hours fantasizing about a thrilling life for herself—breathtaking adventures deep in a jungle or at fancy high-society parties, imaginary scenarios in which she finally played the lead role. Day after day, she would daydream, polishing and editing her own heroic feats. She became an explorer, a freedom fighter, a musician, an exceptional athlete. She saw herself in the caves of the Resistance, on the high seas, in the middle of the desert. Her double life soothed her, reassuring her that one day she would be able to make herself noticed. She would settle into her bed, close her eyes, and lose herself in her own storytelling. When it was time for school she would have to stop, but she could blissfully pick up where she'd left off later that evening.

As a teenager, she finally found a refuge in the real world: mountaineering. She had stumbled on it at random during summer camp and realized that it provided her with exactly what she had been missing: a way to exult in the body she had never liked very much, an outlet for the tenacity and courage she had experienced only in dreams, and a spot on a team in which each member mattered. With her lightness and flexibility, she became very good. The idea of becoming a guide had crossed her mind, but she didn't have the guts to deal with the conflict it would cause in her family:

"That's not a job for a woman. What will you do when you have children?"

It had become a hobby, and it would stay a hobby. Once Louise became an independent adult with a job in Paris, she contented herself with dashing to the train station every weekend, climbing shoes or ice ax and crampons in her bag.

HIGH-SPEED TGV TRAIN, car 16, seats 46 and 47. Ludovic is on his way to join some friends on a ski trip, but after forty-five minutes of playing around on his iPhone, he is beginning to get bored. Next to him, a girl is engrossed in a climbing guidebook. She must be around the same age as he is.

"Do you climb mountains?"

At first she responds grudgingly to this annoying person forcing her to look up from her riveting book, but she is soon won over by his encouraging smile.

She used to try to talk to her colleagues about her passion, but they quickly got bored with her technical jargon and stories about routes and grades, so she retreated again into her own daydreams. Climbing has taken over every nook and cranny of her imagination, but it's an inaccessible subject to most people. She lives for her weekends, and gets through each week with polite indifference. She often looks at the poster of the Aiguille du Dru that she has hung up on the wall of her office. It's her secret—a world that other people can't understand, a world that is hers alone.

But with this pleasant guy next to her, and a window of time on the train that feels removed from reality, she lets herself open up. Gaining confidence from the stranger's nods, she goes a step further and begins to wax poetic. She tells him about seeing the bluish-pink dawn upon leaving the refuge; about the recognizable texture of each kind of rock underneath her fingertips; about nights spent glued to the rock face in a hanging tent called a portaledge, balancing in the wind like a wisp of straw as the light of the valley disappears behind the clouds, feeling like she is closer to the sky than she is to the earth, close to eternity. She tries to convey the beauty of a route that is as simple and as straight as possible, dazzling in its purity. She describes the cracking of the ice crust underneath her feet, the whistling of the rope when it's sent off into the unknown.

He listens to her, amused to find so much passion in this rather ordinary-looking girl. Not to mention her beautiful eyes, green with flecks of gold that sparkle when she is fired up about something.

They say goodbye as they step off the local train in Chamonix. He extends an invitation, mostly to be polite but not without some interest of his own:

"Come by with your friends some night. We go to the Dérapage bar after skiing."

Two days later, Phil, Benoît, and Sam, Louise's climbing partners, are stunned when she suggests that they go get a drink after climbing the Aiguilles Rouges. Usually, they have to drag her to any social outing. The two groups fall into easy conversation. Ludovic is surprised to hear how reverently Louise's three friends talk about her:

"She's the best one. She can do level 7 climbs. There's no one like her when it comes to sensing where there's a crevice."

"She never freaks out when a storm rolls in. She can't get enough."

"She has so much energy even though she's so small. It's incredible."

Out of the corner of his eye, Ludovic looks at Louise, who is at the other end of the table. After the climb, she seems relaxed. With a pretty smile, she is telling the people sitting across from her about a tiny hold that she had just barely managed to grab onto, demonstrating using her hands. Her fingernails are broken. Ludovic supposes she's not quite so ordinary after all.

When he returns to Paris, he is still intrigued, so he calls her and suggests that maybe, if she ever does an easy climb with her friends, she could take him along and guide him through it. Nothing would make her happier. Of course, she already likes him; she's never had the opportunity to seduce anyone so tall and good-looking. Her romantic experience is limited to some adolescent fumbling and a few nights where she hadn't had the courage to say no. It's best to be like everybody else, after all. She's never taken much pleasure in anything that has to do with love, and has persuaded herself that it's not important. Staying single is as good a way as any other to avoid the romantic failures she expects. But this time she feels both flattered and secretly attracted to him. So she tries hard to find some mixed courses that will work for both a beginner and her three friends, who merely exchange knowing smiles with each other: This is it! Their Alpine Virgin Mary has finally fallen for someone!

Six months later, they move in together. Their relationship, which had begun as a vacation fling, quickly fills their bodies and hearts with joy. He makes her laugh; she impresses him. Her energy is sensitive, waiting just under the surface. She seems calm, reserved—timid, even—but transforms when she is climbing or when they make love. Under his touch she cries out, not holding anything back. It's like still water that's ready at any moment to tumble down into a waterfall.

Now that she's gotten over the exquisite surprise of such a good-looking guy being interested in her, Louise loves him for the way he has expanded her life. He embodies the joy and insouciance that she never had when she was a little girl. Sometimes she finds his reactions a little childish, but she knows that fundamentally it's a good thing that he's so upbeat all the time. She'll nestle her head against his shoulder as he enthusiastically talks and makes plans. He brings light into her existence.

Of course Ludovic is the first one to suggest leaving. Maybe he had gotten unlucky at work, or maybe he hadn't been paying close enough attention; either way, he screwed up twice professionally in quick succession. First there was the conference where the food wasn't good—a huge mistake.

And then there was the speaker who turned out to have been a bad choice: he bored the group of managers in the audience to death during an incentive meeting. Ludovic was informed, bluntly, about both of these situations. He decides that the job is a pain in the ass. He had organized paintball games and weekends in Corsica with joyful cynicism, pretending to agree that that was the way to repair any damage done from an overly hasty merger. He had truly gone to great lengths to make sure that the aperitifs were on time, the decorations were perfect, the whole razzle-dazzle. But he's not going to spend his whole life doing that!

Nasty weather in the springtime forces him to start taking the subway instead of his scooter, and one evening, he feels anger bubbling up inside of him. Anger about the amorphous mass of people jolting around in the subway car, each of them with a blank stare and headphones in their ears. Anger about the rancid condensation from their damp bodies that drips down the windows. Anger about the indifference, the sadness, the routine. He looks at the long brown and gray coats, the corners of the mouths turned downward, the hands holding mechanically onto the steel poles. He has the terrible feeling that an outside observer wouldn't see him as being any different from the rest of them.

Of course, he could continue on just like this. One day, his life could include a house in the Gulf of Morbihan, vacations in the Antilles, wine-soaked parties, a managerial role, one or two children. But even this doesn't soothe him. A few times, when he was on a mountain or in the ocean, he has gotten the sense that he is brushing up against what life really is. He remembers fleeting moments in which he has experienced complete concentration, feeling the tips of his fingers shaking on a too-small climbing hold, or vibrating from top to bottom as he surfs a wave. It's not exactly a sensation of transcendence—the term makes him smile—but the feeling that, for at least a moment, he is inhabiting his body completely. At age thirty-three, when he looks back on his life, these are the only moments that are engraved in his memory—in addition, of course, to a few moments of romantic ecstasy. He has to do something, now, and fast. It's do or die.

It takes Ludovic six months to convince Louise. For her, life is good. During the daytime she immerses herself conscientiously in the legal intricacies of the tax collection center; every night, she falls in love with Ludovic all over again. She has happily learned to enjoy dining at little restaurants and going to the movies, spending romantic evenings at home, and even going to crazy parties. On the weekends, they go climbing—he has become a decent climber—or sailing on Ludovic's parents' boat, which she has discovered she enjoys. Why not just wait calmly until her stomach begins to grow round, someday? There's no hurry.

But she senses that she has to give in. He has become sullen, and keeps bringing the subject up again. Finally he employs a strategy that exasperates Louise: he tells their friends that they'll be leaving soon. After that, at every party, one of them says mockingly:

"So, the big day is coming up soon, huh?"

It is the fear of losing him that finally convinces her. After all, what's the risk? They'll have an amazing time on an unforgettable, beautiful trip, and then they'll come back. This is their chance, while they're still healthy and childless: it's now or never. They can't be earnest and responsible forever; they need to live a little, bring some intensity into their lives. This last argument is the one that gets to Louise, reminding her of the heroic adventures she used to dream about. It's what she loves most about climbing—the intensity that forces you to abandon yourself to the sensations of the moment. Ludovic has already brought his warmth and joy into her life. If he hadn't found her, she would have walled herself off completely, fossilized in her own solitude. She knows that at the foot of a dangerous climb it's normal to feel afraid and resist the challenge for a few minutes. It's happened to her before: she had wondered what she was doing there, helmet on her head and ice ax in her hand. But all she needed to do was to concentrate on the technique, and eventually she found herself at the end of the rope, rejoicing in her success. She is sleeping worse and worse, and finally one night, everything becomes very clear: if she doesn't go, if she chickens out and sticks to her routine instead, she'll be angry with herself for the rest of her life. So she wakes up Ludovic so that she can tell him right away that she'll go with him. That way, there will be no way for her to go back on her decision.

They start to negotiate, little by little. She requests that they take only one year of sabbatical and he grants it to her. They'll see how they're doing after that year. Out of the dozens of plans that he suggests to her, they decide against horseback riding across the Andes, biking across New Zealand, and climbing mountains in Pakistan.

The best plan is a boat and a tour of the Atlantic. The most logical route is to start off with an easy trip to the Antilles, to get the hang of things, before descending toward Patagonia—which is supposed to be paradise for ice climbers—and then crossing over to South Africa. In Cape Town they'll decide what to do next. There would still be time to put the boat onto a cargo ship and return sensibly to work. On the other hand, they would also be right next to the Indian Ocean, which would allow them to embark on a tour of the whole world.

They start to argue, sometimes quite sharply, about how to put the plan into action. He makes fun of her for wanting to sail in winter to get used to the bad weather. She calls him irresponsible for claiming that an emergency locator beacon is a waste of money. They're playing tug-of-war, pulling each other one way and then the other. Their trip, which has become a shared dream, is making them starry-eyed with excitement, and neither one can help trying to plan it in exactly the way they have envisioned.

For a year, they haunt boat shows and "Southern Seas Weeks" organized by tour operators. They meet people like the famous Hervé, an experienced veteran of a Patagonia charter, who helps them track down the perfect boat. At first glance they think the sailboat, which looks forlorn in the back of a shipyard in the Vendée, is clumsy and potbellied, but its name, the *Jason*, wins them over. Going on adventures worthy of the boat's mythological name, acquiring their own

Golden Fleece—this is exactly what they are hoping for! Destiny is winking at them. They spend evening after evening with Hervé, analyzing maps, the best anchorages, the pitfalls of katabatic winds. They discuss the wind, the cold, the high seas, icebergs. They collect guides from people Louise knows for climbing routes around Ushuaia that they know they won't have time to visit.

One morning, with an exquisite pang of anguish, they set out on their own, leaving Cherbourg in the clouds behind them. Their partnership is working beautifully—Ludovic sometimes pushes a little too much and Louise not quite enough, but ultimately they support each other. Their life has become full to bursting. As the weeks pass, they dawdle at an anchorage, rejoice at the top of a mountain, battle hand over hand at the helm. Every morning is an adventure, every day is different, and every evening they feel fulfilled by their discoveries and freedom. Their trip isn't just a big vacation. They are finding in it an exultation that is turning into exaltation. The Canary Islands, the Antilles, Brazil, Argentina: the farther they go, the more the world appears to them like a magnificent playground, complex and strange and moving and exhilarating. They love the crumbling azulejo tiles in the alleys of Lisbon; they get soaked through with rain while climbing the twelve-thousand-foot Mount Teide in the Canary Islands; they stuff themselves with dorado while crossing the Atlantic. In the Antilles, they flee the disenchanted marinas in Guadeloupe and Martinique for the charms of Montserrat and a week playing at Robinson Crusoe alone on the infinite beaches of Barbuda. They sing and dance, gasping for breath, pressed up against other bodies amid a crowd of Brazilians in Olinda, and then they mourn the end of Carnival after four days of delirium, sweat, and cachaça. When their cell phone is stolen in Buenos Aires, they laugh, and promise each other that they won't buy a new one. Along the Argentine coast the air is sharper, the sky brighter, and the wind relentless. They take out the oilskin jackets they've brought for rough weather with the delightful sense of having gotten to the hard part. And in fact they have: the next two squalls leave them at the helm with their backs burning with fatigue and their faces white with salt. The storms are frightening enough that entering the Beagle Channel and docking at the ugly floating dock in Ushuaia gives them a feeling of pure happiness. In Ushuaia they meet some of the tanned faces they've seen in magazines, who welcome them as though they are real sailors. They are proud of this. For two months, they gorge themselves on hikes through the jumbled old forests and beautiful treks in the Darwin mountain range, and take to drinking maté and pisco sours, the horrible local drink. They make love on deck one mauve evening, undisturbed but for the rumbling of the glaciers.

There are so many good days and so few bad ones. The indecency of their happiness compared to the rest of the world doesn't cross their minds.

The farther they sail, the tougher they become, gaining experience and confidence. They no longer hesitate when reefing the *Jason*'s sail or hoisting the spinnaker. Louise probably could have realized this, but they have arrived at exactly the level of expertise that climbers know is the most dangerous: when you're experienced enough to try anything, but still too inexperienced to be able to get yourself out of every possible bad situation. When they leave Patagonia for South Africa, they already know that their trip won't be ending there. The Indian Ocean is beckoning to them, and after that, the immense Pacific.

On the way, the forbidden island winks at them. One more adventure . . . Louise protests weakly, but ultimately the two of them decide to take the plunge, with the enthusiasm of kids skipping school.

"A few days, two weeks at most. We're early in the season, so it's the best time to see the baby penguins!"

Yes, they had made all the right decisions, up until that January night.

THEY ARE SITTING side by side, looking out at the bay as if by some miracle there might be something there that has escaped their notice. The only thing they have with them— the backpack set down in between them—seems minuscule. They know exactly what is inside: two ice axes, two pairs of crampons, sixty feet of rope, three climbing nuts just in case, two emergency blankets, the water bottle, the lighter, a box of survival matches, two polar fleeces, the camera, and three granola bars and two apples left over from their dinner the previous night. This is all they have left of the world before.

Finally, Ludovic ventures, "I'm hungry. Aren't you?"

"There are still some apples and granola bars."

Her tone of voice is haughty, biting. She wants to tell him to go to hell. Eating! All he's doing is underscoring how tragic their situation is. That's just like him—irresponsible as always. He's the one who got them into this disaster, and now he wants to have a picnic? But her climbing experience holds her back. It's not the time to start an argument.

"You want any?" he asks her.

"No, I'm not hungry."

Her voice is so icy that Ludovic doesn't dare take their

meager provisions out of the bag. "Go ahead, eat something and make the most of it," he says. "It's the last time."

Louise has been trying to keep herself under control, but now it's a lost cause. "Oh, go ahead, eat now and we'll see what happens later, just like always! Act first and think later!"

Ludovic bristles. "Oh! Little Miss Perfect! I guess we won't even look at the apples! We're going to have to find something to eat anyway, two apples won't make a difference."

"I know, but I've had enough of this shit," she says, fuming. "It's always the same thing with you and it's just this kind of behavior that's gotten us into this mess."

"Hey, I didn't force you to come here! We planned everything together."

Their fear is turning to anger. They're arguing as though everything is normal, as though they're sitting comfortably on their couch at home. Louise is seized with anguish. Not only have they been completely stranded, they've also been sentenced together—with each other or against each other. What couple could survive that type of imprisonment?

Ludovic is coming to the same realization. He still doesn't dare take the food out of the bag; he feels like a guilty little kid, which he finds very annoying. She could be making an effort to stay positive instead of hurling criticism at him.

"Maybe we could go check the base to see if there's still something lying around?" he tries.

"That would surprise me, considering it's been abandoned since the fifties!"

"But we can at least try."

"Okay, we'll try," she concedes.

It takes them several minutes to put their words into action. Both of them still feel dazed, overcome by helplessness and lifeless despair. They have gone numb; their thoughts are a murky, useless swamp. To tear themselves away from their hypnotic contemplation of the empty bay and try to do something, anything, would mean accepting an appalling reality. Breaking out of their despondency requires an effort that's almost painful.

Ludovic is the one to pull them out of their lethargy. His voice is weary. "Let's go."

For two hours they wander around the station, which is really an entire village.

Sidestepping fallen beams, banging sheets of metal, and rotten floorboards, they make their way through rooms once used for processing blubber, carpentry workshops, laboratories.

STROMNESS ISLAND HAS appeared on maps ever since Monsieur de La Truyère, en route to Cape Horn from Brittany in the mid-eighteenth century and forced off course by a nasty series of cyclones, saw snow-topped peaks emerging from the fog like monstrous domes of whipped cream. After that, the island had barely fifty more years of peace before the marauding seal-hunters came to decimate the elephant seal and fur seal populations, their greedy eyes seeing only barrels of valuable blubber. For decades, big ships would anchor in the safest harbors and send their men out to risk their lives roving around in rowboats. By the time the men returned, their boats loaded all the way up to the bulwarks, those who had remained on the flagship had arranged the boilers on the deck. Day and night, the sealers would be up to their knees in oil on one side of the ship and skinning pelts on the other. When all the barrels were full and the hold crammed with soft seal fur, the ship would head back to Europe, often leaving behind the graves of unlucky sailors to vanish beneath the unrelenting blows of the rain and wind.

The nineteenth century marked a shift from the era of traditional seal hunting, with spears and harpoons, to an industrial era of total massacre. Hunters realized that it was more convenient—and above all, more profitable—to build facilities on the island itself to process the carcasses, maintain the ships, and house the men. So they brought entire boats filled with materials to construct factories at the bottom of the world and provide lodging for the poor souls who would have happily traded places with anyone else, even the Midlands coal miners.

Later, as the population of fur seals and elephant seals thinned out, sailors turned their attention—with the help of new technologies—to the whales that were still frolicking around the depths of the bays. Starting around 1880, the permanent structures on the island were transformed into actual villages, although without any women or children. In the winters, small teams would stay to maintain the facilities. In the summers, the waters swarmed with hundreds of fishermen, butchers, stokers, and coopers; in their wake were blacksmiths, carpenters, electricians, mechanics, sailmakers, inspectors, and cooks. There were even several priests, doctors, and tooth pullers. The ships provided everything, from the smallest of screws to food, and they left again filled with "white gold": lamp oil, lubricating oil for fine machinery, skins, baleen, ambergris, meat, bone . . .

The Stakhanovites of the southern latitudes were proud of the hundreds of whales they had killed.

A considerable amount of material accumulated: thousands of tons of wood, scrap metal, machinery, and spare parts, brought to the wild island by the boatful. In response to this well-designed and organized slaughterhouse for sea mammals, other faraway factories and machines sprouted up, creating a global network of perpetual motion. Fur and elephant seals and whales succumbed by the hundreds of thousands. Their paradise had become a mass grave.

But death's work was so effective it got the better of life. The animals vanished, leaving nothing left to hunt. Simultaneously, the development of the petroleum industry, synthetic oils, and plastics relegated whale and seal hunting to museums, alongside the whalebone corsets that women no longer wore.

Between the two wars, the stations began to close. The first measures of species protection were accompanied by the withdrawal of funding from the now-defunct industry. Autumn of 1954 saw the last of the departures. The men fled, leaving behind ghost towns as a testament to their greed—vast junkyards underneath the wide-open sky, with only the wind to erase the traces of their wretched existence.

Exploring the base soothes Louise and Ludovic. They're not quite so alone after all—people have lived here before, and who knows what they have left behind? They wander from workshops to warehouses, awed.

Some of the more intimate places speak to the fragility of the bodies and souls of all those who were here only to work: the dentist's chair; the roughly carved votive offerings in the little chapel; the photo of a woman's face, almost entirely erased by the damp and held up by a rusty thumbtack that looks like a brown teardrop. This place has known shouts, commands, and arguments, but also laughter and moments of celebration. The overall impression is one of infuriating waste. All those pitiful lives and mounds of garbage, and for what—so that people could oil their machines and Paris could call itself the "City of Light"?

Ludovic and Louise aren't in the mood today to philosophize about the inner workings of civilization. They're paying attention only to things that might be old cans or packages of food. After two hours of searching, they find what might be a miracle. Near the shore there is an actual shipyard that still contains one whaling ship, at least twenty meters long and fallen from its cradle; several rowboats; and a collection of propellers that have been eaten away by rust. A building that must have been the office is adjoined by a huge shed that would delight a scrap dealer: hundreds of crates full of new spare parts, entire engines carefully wrapped, racks of metal rods sorted by size, and cabinets of bolts. Especially entrancing are two boxes on a corner of a shelf, inscribed with words that are still visible: "Survival Kit."

They're familiar with the countless stories about the sailors who rowed to the shore in tiny boats to hunt seals on the beach, and the inevitable shipwrecks that resulted. Were the shipowners aware of how dangerous it was? Who was the compassionate official who made these kits—inadequate as they are—obligatory? In each box there are ten packages of sealed tar paper. Inside, under three more layers of paper, is brown, greasy bread. The taste is revolting, somewhere between old flour and rancid oil. Louise nearly vomits, but her stomach demands what her mouth refuses. They each gulp down a half ration, grab the crates, and retreat to their shelter from the night before.

It has started to rain again, this time without wind. The lapping of the water produces a gloomy melody that manages to devastate them both. Ludovic forces himself to find some wood. They relight the fire and stay in front of it for a while, absorbed in the movement of the flames, their only comfort. They feel empty, without willpower or solutions. In these high latitudes, daylight fades infinitely slowly. It requires all of Ludovic's energy to break the silence.

"There must be teams of scientists who come here. It's a nature reserve, so they must study something, I don't know what, the number of albatrosses or penguins. And they must come around now, while the weather's warmer."

"Probably, but where is their base? Clearly it's not here. An island that's one hundred and fifty kilometers long and thirty across, with impassable glaciers between each bay—they could come and leave again without ever seeing us."

"We could catch their attention, put up an SOS on top of the hills, make a flagpole."

"Okay, but they'd better hurry. With what we've got to eat we won't last long."

"So we'll hunt seals and penguins. At this point, what's the use worrying about a fine . . . A little penguin ragout cooked in fat would be edible. It's not like we'd be the first ones to try it."

Louise looks at Ludovic for a long time, staring deep into his eyes as though she'll find there the source of his astonishing optimism.

"I love you."

He wraps his hand around the nape of her neck and they kiss slowly, very slowly, as they had done the very first time they kissed. The tragedy is turning them into different people, they're realizing. They can feel it. Earlier they had argued, but it wasn't important, just a fit of temper caused by the panic that had overtaken them. As long as they are together, their love will support and protect them. That's where their strength lies: a man and a woman united against the thousands of kilometers of watery desert, against solitude, against death. Allowing themselves to be overcome by a desperate need for each other, they curl up in the run-down bed and make love gently, driven more by the tenderness of a parent rocking their child's cradle than the passionate frenzy of lovers.

B Y FOUR A.M., it is already light outside. Louise is tempted to snuggle up to her giant and fall back asleep—to close her eyes and hope that magically, when she awakens, it will be twenty-four hours in the past and everything will turn out okay. But no. She spirals into thinking about the little things that can cause major consequences: several more meters of chain, a gust of wind in a slightly different location . . .

Ludovic stirs, his sleep disturbed by the light. He, too, is thinking. They have to face the situation. They're young, smart, healthy. Many people have survived conditions much worse. They had gone off in search of adventure, and here it is—the real kind of adventure, the kind that reveals you to yourself. They have to rise to the challenge. For a minute, he imagines himself one day in the future giving a motivational talk to an adoring audience, who jump to their feet in a standing ovation . . .

But this isn't the time to daydream. He pushes back the covers.

T HUS BEGINS THEIR Robinson Crusoe life. They wake up at dawn and bustle around, full of energy. Their arguments seem to be behind them. The whole ordeal, they think, will bring them closer.

The base is a formidable workshop. If they need a hammer, a pair of pliers, or a piece of wood or sheet metal, they just have to go to the "store." They fix up a makeshift stove by clearing an opening in the shape of a fireplace and punching air holes in a two-hundred-liter can. They manage to fit together a pipe to use on top as a chimney, which goes up through the roof through a hole they create by breaking a tile. This creates an air current, but the smoke no longer reddens their eyes and irritates their throats. Their achievement fills them with optimism. They repair the door, collect a better mattress, and track down tin plates, a table, and chairs. Later, they will realize that throwing themselves into action like this had been a kind of denial. At this point, they don't truly believe that they have been abandoned. Unconsciously, they are living with the belief that someone will come; it's merely a matter of days, perhaps weeks at the very most. They are playing house like kids waiting for the dinner bell to ring. But all the same, these activities allow them to keep up morale. Staying busy reassures the couple, keeping their fear at arm's length.

During the next several days, they venture to the outskirts of the bay, choose a hill that faces the open sea, and use stones to make a gigantic SOS on it with an arrow that points to where they are staying. It is exhausting work. They have to find the whitest, flattest stones, which often need to be violent dislodged with an iron rod, and then drag the stones up the hill. They work with their heads down, instinctively keeping their backs to the open sea, conscious that the empty horizon, enlivened only by swells and erratic icebergs, is an outright denial of their hope of rescue. From the top of the hill they scan the next bay, just to be sure that the *Jason* isn't there, lying on its flank. But there is nothing but more cliffs, water strewn with pieces of ice, and intertwining streams that give the impression of a silvery net lost on the beach. They note with satisfaction that there are an extraordinary number of penguins. The shore is black, a carpet of feathers; the sea spits out and swallows a steady flow of the animals; the hills seem to be alive with Brownian motion. There must be tens of thousands of them.

"Well, looks like our pantry is full!" jokes Ludovic.

The penguins are a major undertaking. Despite a thorough exploration of the base, they haven't found anything else to eat, and have quickly become tormented by the combination of hunger and the fear of exhausting their food supply. The solution, it turns out, is the ungainly and peaceful penguin. It takes them a little while to fine-tune their technique. At first they try to chase after them, but the birds always end up finding their way back to the sea and disappearing. In the end, the most successful technique consists of cutting off all possible retreats and slowly herding a group toward a corner, taking care not to scare them, and then beating the pile with heavy iron rods. The birds topple without a scream. From time to time one of the birds tries to bite their legs, but an angry kick finishes the animal off. They aim for the king penguins, which stand almost a meter tall and have more meat than the little gentoo, macaroni, or chinstrap penguins. Neither Louise nor Ludovic experiences any remorse. Sometimes they even feel overcome with morbid

pleasure in being able to kill with such ease. Earlier, they
had exclaimed over the charming black heads topped with
a splash of brilliant orange. They had been moved by the
sight of the parents feeding their children, had laughed at
their solemn waddle. But that had been in another life, when
they were just passing by. Now they are part of this ecosys-
tem, and like any predator, they must take what they need.

Plucking the birds is an experience. It's impossible to
plunge them into boiling water, the method Louise's grandmother used to talk about. Their attempts to rip off the
feathers tear the skin and leave bits of feathers behind that
stick to the roofs of their mouths when they eat. Finally, they
learn to skin them, although they are sorry to lose so much
of the good fat in the process. Despite its size, even a king
penguin doesn't make for a particularly abundant meal. Once
it's skinned, all that remains are the two wing joints on each
side of the wishbone, which resemble chicken breasts with a
strong stench of fish. They boil them in a mix of fresh water
and salt water, for flavor, and pretend to amuse themselves
by giving fancy names to their meager rations: "small éminčé
of breast without sauce," "carcass broth with leftover meat."

Ludovic had read that the local cabbage was a powerful
antiscorbutic, but it tastes so strong it burns their mouths
like hot pepper. In order to eat it they have to boil it in
several changes of water, but this is time-consuming and
requires a lot of wood. And anyway, there isn't much of it
growing near the base. Next they try the long kelp that covers the rocks, and they gather limpets. This isn't very nour-

ishing and all of it still tastes like damn fish. At a rate of four penguins per person per day, they can alleviate their hunger, but there aren't that many of the animals in their bay.

So they decide to go on a refueling expedition to the cove they've discovered. On a nice day, they sail out in the dinghy, rowing instead of using the motor to conserve gas, and spend three hours traveling around the part of the island that juts out to the west of them. Even far offshore, they are assaulted by the smell of waste and rotting fish. On the beach, the din is deafening. The birds are returning from hunting, their crops swollen with a mash of fish ready to be regurgitated and fed to their chicks. The arriving birds are able to recognize their offspring only through each bird's individual vocalization, so they wander around squealing, pecking the unwanted little birds to chase them away, until they find their families. Once they do, the parent who had stayed to incubate the chicks steps away, and one or two little brown fuzzballs run to attach themselves to the newcomer, beaks wide open. Here and there, sheathbills as white as doves nibble at the waste, and predatory skuas circle overhead at low altitude, ready to seize a stray or sickly chick.

Louise has moved slowly into the middle of the colony, the sea of feathers opening to make way and then closing again behind her. In this little humanoid society, everyone attends to their own business—taking care of their offspring, reprimanding them with a peck, stealing their neighbor's pebbles for their own nest, arguing with each other, courting each other. Some of them seem to just be walking around, their black eyes eternally stunned or thoughtful. The overall impression is that of a sort of warm throng of bodies. Louise has tears in her eyes without knowing exactly why. Is it just the sight of these fragile lives carrying on at the icy outskirts of the world? Or, more profoundly, is it nostalgia for a crowd, for a mass of other people to share things with or defend yourself against? For a minute she envies the penguins, feeling deeply alone.

A chorus of squawking distracts her from her meditation. Ludovic has rushed to attack the colony with the greed of unsatisfied hunger. Every twirl of his stick knocks out several birds, and their neighbors flee, protesting. He hits and hits, his movements imbued with a frenzy that's almost vile. Louise, watching this awful man murdering with all his might, feels a flash of hatred.

Barely lifting his head, he shouts at her:

"Come on, don't just stand there! Get them in the dinghy and stop the others from running into the water."

Rousing herself from her torpor, she does as he asks. Half an hour later, the little boat is loaded with about a hundred of the animals, a silky black-and-white mountain whose wet feathers glisten in the sun.

"Stop!" she yells at him. "We're already going to have trouble getting back with this load. And then we'll have to take them all out."

"It's not like we'll be back here all the time," protests Ludovic, returning to his task.

Finally, he assesses the pile that is covering the entire dinghy.

"Okay, let's go. I guess now we know the route to the pantry."

The way back proves to be distinctly more hazardous than the way there had been. They are sitting on a pile of dead meat that's slipping and sliding underneath them. Louise feels like she can hear the flesh getting crushed and the bones breaking. Rowing requires all their energy. The choppy waves and sideways current toss around the over-loaded boat, covering them with sea spray. After an hour, they have to shift the cargo in order to bail out the boat, and in the process several animals slip into the water. For the first time since the *Jason* disappeared, they argue.

Louise, whose shoulder pain has returned due to the row-ing, has been gritting her teeth, but after another hour, they realize that the wind is really picking up and that it will be difficult for them to reach the shore.

"Start the motor," she begs. "We're not going to get there."

"No! We can't waste the gas. Imagine if we see a boat pass—we have to be able to get to it."

They spend another ten minutes trying to row, getting more and more worked up. Finally Ludovic angrily hits the pile of dead birds with his oar.

"Shit!"

The sound of the motor—the sound of civilization—soothes them. Closing their eyes, they can almost make themselves believe that they're returning from a nice walk, going back to their dear *Jason* to snuggle up under a cozy duvet or sit down to a nice meal.

When they reach land, they still need to transport all their cargo to the ground floor of the shack they're staying in so that they can get it out of the rain that has, of course, decided to start falling. Soaked and exhausted, they barely have the energy to relight their fire, skin their four daily penguins, and wait close to an hour for the water to boil and the birds to cook. Usually, Louise insists that they both wash up, meaning sponge themselves down with lukewarm water and an old rag, before going to sleep. Tonight, though, they crawl right into bed, their clothes and hands still soaked with blood and stuck-on feathers. A deep sleep prevents them from hearing the racket that has commenced on the floor below.

But in the morning, when they go downstairs to take on the task of skinning all the animals, the sound of their footsteps sends hordes of rats, who had been feasting all night, scattering. It's carnage. The penguins have been dragged in all directions through the mud, leaving behind viscera, bits of skin, eyes that have been gnawed at. The pile of birds that they had so painstakingly gathered seems to have exploded from within, oozing slimy clumps. As they approach, one last rat darts out from the very heart of the bloody mass, its white teeth gleaming against its black fur glistening with mucus and blood. They scream in unison.

All that for this! Their exhausting trip, the massacre, just to feed these disgusting creatures! Through the dirty window, the sun beams down on three penguins that have been spared. Lying one against the other, their eyelids closed, it looks like they're sleeping. Louise has the urge to take them in her arms and cradle them. She breaks down in tears.

"Louise, this isn't the time to fall apart."

Ludovic had rushed toward the bolting rat, but now he turns back to the pile of penguins and plunges his hand in, furiously sorting the birds that are still intact from the ones that aren't and throwing the damaged ones to the side. "Why don't you come over here instead of just standing there!"

She joins him, sniffling, and they spend their day sorting, skinning, and hanging the bodies on a rail that is out of reach for the rats. They save only forty or so. Then they have to collect and throw out the other carcasses and clean up as well as they can so that the rodents won't come right back. It's a tedious chore; they have to go fetch water from the stream a hundred meters away and sweep with a broom that's missing half its bristles. They work without speaking, each of them silently blaming the other for the disaster.

Toward the end of the afternoon, Louise leaves to go find some limpets to vary their menu. She needs to extricate herself from this nauseating task. The tide is low and the dark sand gleams; the wind is scrunching up the waves in plumes of smoke and turning the bay white. She is cold and feels miserable and abandoned. Until today, she had kept her memories of her life before at a distance, concentrating on the hope of survival. She had been convinced that together, they would be capable of getting out alive. But all of a sudden she's no longer sure. She pictures her fifth-floor office at the tax center: the gray desk, the plastic storage bins, the computer, the wilting green plant, the poster of the Drus, the smell of coffee in the hallway, the sharp voices of her colleagues beyond glass doors—the colleagues who at this very moment might be envying her for lazing around in the sun. All of this comes back to her in a flash, causing her chest to clench. A paradise forever lost. She resists picturing their apartment, the cozy nest that they had so stupidly left behind. Why did she give in to Ludovic? It was her own fault; she should have been firmer. She had been afraid of losing him, but now they're both at risk of losing themselves as well as each other. He's still acting reckless. If they had brought back fewer animals, they would have been able to row back comfortably and still have time to store the animals safely.

As she ponders this, she is pulling up algae, and she finally smiles when she spots two little fish abandoned by the tide in a rock crevice. Then it occurs to her that these poor trapped fish are just like her and Ludovic, and that the fish will quickly be devoured by a skua or a seagull. Is their own future any different?

By the time she returns, Ludovic has started a fire and is sawing wood with the same contained fury as before, sending sawdust flying. He has been thinking, too. In such a merciless environment they need to move faster, act more aggressively. He senses that Louise is indecisive and frightened. This latest disappointment has been a learning experience. They need to return to the penguin colony and figure out how to manage without using the motor. And why not go after the fur and elephant seals? He will become a new man, a tougher and fiercer one; he will fight, fight, fight.

He repeats the word to himself like a mantra as he saws more and more violently.

A storm brews between the two of them that evening. It reaches a breaking point when Louise wants to wash her dirty jacket and pants.

"What, you want to fetch even more water?" Ludovic asks angrily. "Plus, it will waste the wood we need for heat."

"We have plenty of wood, and I'm the one who went to get water before. I have no intention of smelling disgusting in addition to being starving."

He explodes. She hasn't made any effort to adapt. There's no way that the other people who survived living here were this squeamish. He recounts the penguin disaster in exacting detail to prove to her that they could have done things differently if they had had more energy. The stove that provides their only light gives him a reddish glow, making him seem even angrier. As he always does when he is worked up, he communicates with his hands as much as with his words, and his gesticulating shadow on the wall looks like an evil djinni. Watching him, Louise notices how much his big hands have changed in just a few days. They're covered with bumps and scratches, and they're swollen, the knuckles and veins bulging so much they almost look deformed. There are red splotches on his wrists from the constant chafing of his wet, dirty jacket. Fishermen in the old days had called these "sea blisters."

The island has already made its mark on their flesh, and it's only the beginning. What will happen if they get sick? Will their poor diet make them weak? Winter will come . . .

Half listening to him, she watches the steam rising from the clothes that are currently drying, a sort of light fog that dissipates when it reaches window height thanks to the draft. But then he says something that goes too far:

"Come on! You have to trust me."

It's as though one small falling stone has caused the whole wall to come crashing down. She hadn't wanted to get angry, to rehash things that happened in the past or harp on the same criticisms, but the words that she held back for too long are tumbling out of her mouth—harsh words, nasty and bitter, like she's never spoken aloud before. Trust? Who's the one who had dragged them on this useless trip? Made them leave behind their peaceful life to prove God-knows-what to themselves? Decided, in an act of bravado, to come to this island? Insisted on continuing their stupid walk even when the bad weather rolled in? To what point is she supposed to trust him? Until they die here, starving and frozen in this wretched rathole? All her fear, her regrets, her despair, her hunger, the cold, and their lack of a future add to her anger. The time for fun is over; their modern and dynamic relationship is over. There's nothing but two people and the death that patiently awaits them. Her voice shakes, squeaks, grows shrill. The more she talks, the more she realizes that she's completely unable to gain control over herself. Reason tells her that she needs to temper her anger and preserve the essential harmony that they had maintained since the storm. Her outburst is an early defeat, the first crack in the pact they had made to remain optimistic.

Ludovic is frozen, stunned by the tidal wave he has provoked. He likes to be a little polemical because he knows that she'll always be a moderating force. He's even made it a strategy, a game—always exaggerating so that he can win some ground. But Louise's voice, twisting out of control, makes it clear that the game is over. She is shouting like a crazy person, stammering with anger. The newfound angularity of her face and her filthy hair glued to her scalp make her body seem even thinner and more fragile, but paradoxically make her merciless speech even more forceful. She is throwing in his face his lack of character, his mediocrity, his stupidity. Has she thought all of this ever since they started dating? What is she even doing with him if he's so worthless? Are this island and this whole situation turning them insane? He fixes his eyes on the ground, dazed. He has lost his footing. The trust he had in their fate has splintered, and this realization uses up all his strength.

Louise's voice finally cracks into a sob, and she stops speaking. They stay there, exhausted, sitting one in front of the other, surrounded by a silence that seems unreal. Tonight there isn't any wind to torment the base and the house. Just silence, as though they weren't even there—as though the island has already swallowed them up.

THEIR LIFE TOGETHER resumes. They don't have a choice. Continuing to argue would require energy and desire they don't have. Mostly what they feel is remorse for having crossed a line. The night before, after lying on the floor next to the fire for a while, they got into bed, where they were pressed up against each other because of how small it was. Finally, wordlessly, they embraced, or rather they sort of burrowed into each other as if to ward off the fears that had been triggered by their argument. Upon waking, by unspoken agreement, they decide to make an effort to get along. Nothing has been fixed; words have been spoken that will never be forgotten. But they have to pretend, because the prospect of solitude is even worse than the prospect of disagreement. Their relationship has become like a porcelain plate, something that has to be cared for fastidiously. They begin to punctuate all their actions and decisions with an "Okay with you?" or a "Sound good?," exaggerating their mutual good intentions to an almost laughable extent.

It helps that the weather is beautiful for a whole week. Their distress doesn't go away, but it softens. Their surroundings seem less hostile. Every morning they wake up to a calm sun. The reddish colors of the base that had entranced them their first day have returned. The bright sunlight highlights lacy patterns of rust that contrast with the absolute blue of the sky. The old wood looks silver rather than gray. In the light you can see in detail the extraordinary jumble of ruins, the collapsed buildings and the enormous tanks that look as though a giant has picked them up and dropped them violently. Everything is piled on top of each other at awkward angles. The sudden emergence of a wooden plank here or a piece of metal there seems to defy time. In the sheltered hollows of this junkyard are fluorescent green mosses, bright yellow lichens, and clumps of pale mauve acaena that break up the otherwise two-tone world of ocher and gray. In the bay, the water is emerald green near the shore but black at its deepest points, reflecting perfectly the brown cliffs and the snow-topped peaks as though it is a mirror. Their island is radiant, and despite their dismay, they savor its fleeting beauty. All is silent, punctuated only by the call of a penguin, the chirping of a tern in its burrow, or the belching of an elephant seal—the reassuring sounds of their austral barnyard.

In the middle of the day, it becomes almost hot, and they work in T-shirts. Dedicating all their time to finding food makes them feel like they've returned to the Stone Age. After five days, the birds that they had brought back from their first expedition are covered in mold and starting to stink. Determined, they return to the cove, more calmly this time, and bring back fifty or so animals. They slice the breast meat around the birds' flying muscles thinly. Laying the meat out in fresh air, sheltered from the sun and from feathered or furred predators in a cage covered with wire mesh, helps it to begin drying out and turning black. They're proud of having figured out a solution and feel like they have already started to build up a real supply of food.

But their major success is when they manage to attack a fur seal. Until now they have avoided the aggressive animals, who are in their breeding season. Hervé had warned them:

"Those guys are like pit bulls! They'll come charging, and they can move faster than you can. If one bites you, you'll need a medical evacuation. It causes a nasty infection."

He had been right to warn them. At first sight, these beautiful animals, with their silky brown-beige fur, big mustaches, tiny ears, and lovely black eyes, make you want to caress them. Ludovic and Louise quickly notice that the groups spend their time bickering, the females defending their babies and the aggressive males displaying a tendency to confuse, in their vindictiveness, humans with rival seals. So they stay at a distance. During the whaling era, the seals had been practically exterminated for their skins, which were turned into chic and warm coats. Ever since they had become a protected species, the seals had taken over the island again, judging by the sounds and smells. But a fur seal, even a young one, guaranteed dozens of kilograms of meat, as well as oil that Ludovic planned on using to light the lamps.

So one morning, they avail themselves of the forge to sharpen up some antique larding needles, formerly used to carve up whales, and set off on their mission. They're picturing the illustrations from adventure stories in which the hunter heads off brandishing his spear and returns proudly with his catches dangling off a stick. But it will take a lot to turn a tax auditor and an account manager into trappers. First of all, they are scared. With the penguins, they weren't scared at all; killing a bird isn't a big deal. But now, for the first time in their life, they are going to attack a massive living being, a mammal not so different from them. The seal will defend itself, and there's no guarantee that they will win. The possibility of hand-to-hand combat fills them with anxiety and disgust. Physical courage can be learned only from experience, and even Ludovic never fought very much as a kid on the playground. They discuss strategy endlessly but end up retreating whenever it's time to put their words into action. As soon as the seal rears up, growling, they run away, hearts thumping.

Finally, they pick out a little female in a corner. As soon as she sees them, she charges at them, letting out her characteristic nasal groan. The time for philosophizing is over. Ludovic delivers a major blow to her chest and Louise strikes her in the back of her head. Two red geysers spurt out, and the animal whines, disconcerted. Before she can recover, Ludovic and Louise each hit her again, their violent, erratic motions guided by fear. The seal tries weakly to struggle before she collapses all at once, her fur soaked with blood. They wait to be sure that she is dead before they take hold of her, trembling with relief and pride.

Skinning the animal is no easy feat—the skin turns to shreds under the knife—but they collect strips of fat and pieces of very red meat that make their mouths water. When they finish, they are coated with mucus and blood from head to toe.

This sudden influx of food makes them feel better. Granted, fur seal tastes terrible, and their meat-only diet is causing them painful digestive distress, but at least their fear of hunger isn't so strong anymore. That evening, as clouds in the shape of long feathers—harbingers of changing weather—cover the sky, they sit shoulder to shoulder at the top of the beach, leaning against an old piece of sheet metal. The warm sun splashes light onto the icebergs in the distance; the bay is calm; the summer evening softens the ruins and makes the traces of mica in the sand sparkle like flakes of gold. The apparent serenity gives them the courage to think about their argument and finally put it to rest. Ever since they had found the *Jason* gone, they had taken things one day at a time to ensure they had food and shelter. Sometimes, one or the other of them would be woken up by the wind or the uncomfortableness of the bed and plunge into a pit of anguish. Not sharing those thoughts with each other was one way to push them away. Focusing on day-to-day actions and trying to keep their brains empty of any thought of the future served as a strategy. Today, survival seems likely. Slowly, they are accepting the obvious: their stay might very well last for a long time. Ludovic broaches the subject with a joke, in keeping with his usual character:

"We're going to have to find some different recipes for all this meat. I've had enough boiled penguin wings!"

The thought of a tomato salad creeps into Louise's mind.

"Do you think this will last a long time? Will we be spending the winter here?"

She folds herself into her favorite position, bringing her knees to her chest and hugging her legs as though to ward off the freezing temperatures to come.

"Someone must be coming by . . . a research vessel . . ."

"Come on, it's the end of January. If they were going to come to take some kind of census, they would have done it in the summer. They'd already have been here."

"It's possible that they're making the rounds and will finish here, or in James Bay, where the colony of penguins is. We'll see them pass by."

Instinctively they both look out to sea. The horizon is clear—the tiniest bit misty, but hopelessly deserted.

"We could very well miss them. They might pass by at night and not see our message on the hill," Louise insists.

"No, no one would walk around at night here. If you want, we could also leave a message in James Bay."

This reasoning doesn't satisfy Louise. It leaves too much to chance, to the caprices of fate.

"We could try to go find them," she perseveres. "Their base must be in the east. It can't be in the west—there are only cliffs and inaccessible glaciers over there."

"You're nuts. Between each bay there's an 'inaccessible' glacier, like you say, and the island is almost a hundred and fifty kilometers long. We would never reach the base. At least here we have shelter, and we know where to find food. We have to stay—there's no other choice."

From their corner of the coast, they can't see the high

summits. When they had first approached the island on the *Jason*, they had admired the vast and immaculate ice cap that was sprinkled with peaks and ice needles. From the top flowed white-blue rivers, glaciers that divided up the island like slices of an orange. At the time, Louise had quivered with pleasure at the thought of all these "firsts"; now, though, she is evaluating the difficulty of attempting to climb them with little equipment and even less food.

"So that means that we might be spending the winter here."

At last, Louise has spoken the words aloud. A long winter of coldness, nighttime, and storms awaits them. As though to illustrate what she has said, the daylight fades. The fuchsia horizon becomes mauve, then gray, and seems to freeze. How is it possible that, in the age of the internet—when everyone is findable, tracked, recorded—they could be so isolated and so alone? How could this part of the planet be so out of reach?

Before leaving, they had thought about bringing a positioning beacon so that their family and friends could track their location with a computer and an access code. But Ludovic had gotten angry, arguing that what they wanted was to live freely, away from any Big Brothers, even those who were family. And with a beacon, their jaunt to this forbidden island wouldn't have been possible. They had wanted all of this. Freedom, safety, and responsibility are the three points of an impossible triangle. They had leaned toward the first, convinced that the other two would follow—that skill would protect them, always and everywhere. But the facts remain stubborn, and reality—terrible, indifferent reality—has the last word. When they had dreamed about their adventures, they had assumed that, at any given moment, they would have access to a satellite telephone, a robust bank account, or a smoothly functioning rescue system to put a stop to any danger before it was too late.

Their distance from the rest of the world is what they find most devastating, even more than their solitude. How much time will they spend here? Six months, eight months? And what if nobody comes next year? Are they going to spend the rest of their lives filthy and cold, felling animals and skinning them like cavemen? Until death comes for them? The walls of their austral prison are closing in on them.

"Well, I'll go, then. To the scientific base," suggests Louise. "There are still some fifteen-hour days. I'll get there quickly. We have the crampons and the ice axes, and I'll bring some dried seal and penguin. You stay here. We'll double our chances. And I'm sure there will be some communication equipment there—a radio, a satellite telephone."

"It's way too dangerous!" he cries. The prospect of staying alone is unbearable to him.

"Anyway," he continues, "we need both of us to hunt and to maneuver the dinghy. And imagine if you fell and hurt yourself. Listen, the worst-case scenario is that we'll spend the winter here. If no one comes, both of us will go look for the base in the spring together."

They argue a little longer, but deep down, Louise is scared

to leave on her own. She has never tried climbing without the security of a partner.

Night falls. In the last glimmers of light, the old buildings are pale and threatening. A cold wind blows in from the west; a piece of metal screeches. They retreat to their shelter.

PARADOXICALLY, THEIR DECISION to spend the winter here frees them. They're not just sitting around waiting anymore. Now they can think of their future as a plan to be made, something to work toward: they will get organized for the winter and find a means of escape.

They're seized with the frenetic impulse to fix up the building they're staying in. It has to be a real house now, not just a shack they use for shelter. They call it "Number 40," after the number of their building on rue d'Alleray in the fifteenth arrondissement of Paris. On the ground floor, they get the kitchen up and running again and use it to prepare their kills. They hang up some wire to store their precious food out of reach of rodents. Upstairs, the large unoccupied bedroom becomes "the workshop." A table made out of a door laid on top of some bricks becomes their worktable. Also in the room are their wood stockpile, hunting implements, knives, whetstone, iron rods that they use as bludgeons, and old jute bags for collecting shellfish and algae. The holy of holies—the supervisor's former attic room—is simply "the bedroom." They often wander among the ruins, picking up pieces of scrap iron and wood. They're surprised by all the things that they would have considered junk a few months ago that they now consider treasures. In what must have been a laboratory for inspecting oil quality, they unearth several bottles, thick-bottomed glass flasks and pots, and copper bowls streaked with gray and green. Laboriously, they melt the blubber from the fur seal, and fix up cloth wicks to make oil lamps.

Inside the bedroom, the floor is covered with rags for insulation. To the left of the door, two whale vertebrae in front of the stove serve as stools, and they can cover the window at night with something akin to a curtain. Across the room, a series of shelves holds the day's food, the mountaineering equipment, tools, nails, and screws. Underneath the shelves they have squeezed in the old desk, now being used as a table, and two chairs. In the corner to the right, the bed is protected from drafts by a kind of moth-eaten fabric canopy that makes them feel safer when they're going to sleep. All of it reeks of smoke, rancid fat, and dampness, but they don't even notice it anymore. It has become their smell, the smell of their life.

After killing the fur seal, they had believed they had solved the problem of food. But this is far from the truth. When the weather was nice and dry, the meat had just about dried out, too, but it begins to rot again at the slightest hint of moisture in the air. They have to throw out more than half of it after nearly poisoning themselves. For two days they had crawled around vomiting. Next, they try smoking the meat, either outside or in the kitchen when the weather is bad. It works, sort of, but it requires a lot of wood and long hours of keeping the fire going. These difficulties engender never-ending discussions about how people in the olden days—all those pioneers and adventurers they had read about—had done it. Are the two of them particularly useless? What kind of knowledge was lost once food shortages were no longer an issue? Did they just have the bad luck to have come across an island that's not as rich in natural resources? The way they remember it, the Robinsons and others of their ilk didn't spend all their time searching for food. Recollecting the descriptions of the seals that collected hundreds of albatross or penguin eggs, they conclude that the wildlife now must be scarcer, thanks to the excessive hunting of their predecessors. It crosses their minds that in France, too, there's no longer much hunting and fishing, certainly not enough to feed a population, and that population would be equally incapable of preserving the food in salt or sand like their forebears had done.

Their other conclusion is that people in the past must have eaten little and badly, while the two of them have always taken food for granted. Hunger is now with them all day and wakes them up during the night. Their stomach cramps and watering mouths are a source of constant tension and frustration, sometimes causing their eyes to well up with tears. They don't get used to it; hunger follows them everywhere, a little or a lot depending on the day, insidious and impossible to ignore. A steaming plate of potatoes with just a pat of butter and a pinch of salt! Sausage with herbs, seared on the grill! Pasta with ham! Thinking about these wonderful foods only makes their cravings worse. Then they realize, horrified, that even the memory of how these common foods taste is gone. Their gustatory world has shrunk to include only fish with varying levels of rancidness, birds that taste like fish, seals that taste like fish. Everything else is just words.

They are growing thin. Ludovic's muscles are visibly dwindling away, making him appear even taller. Louise, on the other hand, who didn't have much weight to lose to begin with, seems to get smaller and smaller, shriveling up as though her limbs are struggling to hold her. She often gets dizzy but doesn't dare to mention it.

The days get shorter. The weather becomes gloomy, the sky almost always gray and swollen with dark pouches that burst open with torrential rain. They dream of calm days, but every morning from their bed they hear the wind growling in the corners of the house and the lapping of heavy rain. It becomes more and more dangerous to row to James Bay in their flimsy boat, as they have to navigate around the long stretch of coastline that juts out into the ocean, exposing themselves to the breaking swell. But they've killed off all the penguins in their near vicinity, so they have to try to reach James Bay by land. If they follow the coast, they come up against huge cliffs damp with moss. If they stick to the interior, it significantly lengthens their trip. They go up the valley that they had followed the first day; veer off to the right, making use of their feet and hands to navigate the loose stones; come back down toward a little river; and climb up again to go through a mountain pass, where they are exposed to the wind. Finally, they must face a hundred and fifty meters of perilous descent down the flank of a cliff before they reach the penguins. On the way back, loaded up with dead animals, they slip and slide on the wet rocks and rip their jackets on the sharp teeth of the crags. Including an hour of hunting, it takes them seven hours round-trip, and they return to Number 40 completely drained, with at most thirty birds.

One of their most noteworthy achievements comes from their discovery of old notebooks in the laboratory. Entire pages covered with uniform handwriting: columns of numbers reporting on killing sprees, butchering quality control, and metric tons of blubber that will one day become a nice sum of money. The pages are warped, speckled with spots of brown and rust. Mildew has left exploding rosettes of blue, pink, green. These treasures remind them of the old days—reams of crisp, white paper that they'd waste by scribbling a few doodles on a sheet and then tossing it gracefully into the trash can. Ludovic thinks back to the stacks of unused handouts that would be thrown out by the box. Louise longs for the sophisticated notebooks she used to use for her journals, notebooks with fussy, bulky, textured granite paper that made her thoughts seem equally refined. Paper now seems like a technological marvel. They fashion a sort of pen with a sharpened stick and create something like ink by mixing soot and fat. It's crude, but it allows them to write down little notes. Using the backs of the sheets of paper, they begin a journal, arguing over what they think the date is. It becomes an evening ritual for them to record the tasks they had completed that day, using as few words as possible so that they can conserve the paper.

Feb 6: finished the workshop table.

Feb 12: killed 32 penguins, started smoking them
in the kitchen.

Feb 21: lost 10 rotten penguins, collected a bag of
algae and 3 handfuls of limpets.

Feb 23: broke the blade of the good knife, killed a
female fur seal.

However modest their entries, the journal does them a world of good. It gives them a history again, and brings them closer to a normal, civilized life. True, they do have a tendency to report their victories rather than their defeats and their plans rather than their doubts. Unconsciously, they are letting themselves imagine that someday, someone will read it, and they want to make a good impression. Sometimes one or the other has the desire to claim credit for one of their accomplishments, but they have sworn to themselves that they won't ever do it, out of solidarity . . .

Nonetheless, both dream of having their own journal to use as an outlet.

In the evenings, huddled up in the corner of their glowing tin-can house, they tell each other fragments of the stories they remember—the expeditions of Shackleton, Nordenskjöld, and other great polar explorers. Sometimes these stories seem galvanizing and inspiring, giving them endless confidence in the human ability to overcome hardship; other times, though, the stories only make them despair about how clumsy and weak they are in comparison to the heroes. They also try to distract themselves by reconstructing novels, historical facts, and geography. Louise prides herself on her bookishness, but she can't seem to remember the details of *Alice in Wonderland*, or what happens in *Madame Bovary* or *The Red and the Black*. Ludovic gets mixed up when trying to list the kings of France or draw a map of Africa. All these things that they'd learned already seem so far away, nearly useless. They're part of their culture, part of what's supposed to help them fit in with society, but are they at all relevant here? Will they help them find food, or keep them from getting sick? On the other hand, trying to remember these things is a way to not give in to despair, to stay connected to the rest of the human world that they are missing so much. Staying "normal" is an obligation, a viaticum for resistance.

They don't tell each other this, but the things from the world before that float to the surface of their consciousness most often are the most childish ones—nursery rhymes that they are surprised to find themselves humming, memories of a walk with a grandfather, the smell of chocolate pudding. Neither one dares to admit to these nostalgia trips, but they help keep them going.

They decide to institute a set of rules, principles, and rhythms for their daily life to prevent themselves from getting careless. In the mornings they force themselves to jump out of bed at dawn, perform some stretches under Louise's guidance, and then discuss their to-do list for the day. In the evenings, they can eat dinner only after they've completed all their tasks. Thanks to their ineptitude, they often have to keep working into the night, under the fuliginous light of the oil lamps. They take turns fetching water and maintaining the fire, not only during the day but during the night, too, so they can conserve their lighter.

They even establish sanctions for whoever doesn't fulfill their obligations. Louise is inspired by the memory of her family's December ritual. Her parents would take out a wooden board with three columns of twenty-four holes each, one column for each child. Every evening, taking into account the children's actions that day, both good and bad, their parents would move stars fastened onto nails either up or down the board. The idea was that Santa Claus, before leaving his presents, would check that each kid had gotten their star to the top of the board and therefore deserved their reward. Needless to say, the kids always got their stars to the top of the board, accepting any chore they could when the deadline grew nearer so that they could advance at double speed. Ludovic finds this childish, but to make Louise happy, he agrees. In the evenings, after washing up, they meticulously divide up the food into chipped bowls. They have agreed that Ludovic, who is taller, should get one spoonful extra. Part of the night is spent debating their respective accomplishments that day, the results of which are displayed by two rusty nails climbing up a rotten plank. Sundays are the days of reckoning: the loser gets stuck with fetching water one extra time.

Louise insists on not working on Sundays. All productive activities—hunting, fishing, making tools—are forbidden;

it's a kind of austral "Lord's day," incongruous as that is for the two miscreants. They lie around in bed, making love distractedly, taking care to prevent pregnancy, and they grant themselves a mouthful each of emergency rations. If they do go out on Sundays, it's only to walk around, going up the valley like they had done on their walk that first day. If it rains, Louise immerses herself in trying to tan penguin skins, scraping the dermis meticulously to soften it. Ludovic whittles driftwood, shaping it into a clumsy bestiary.

Little by little, these rituals begin to border on superstition. Abandoning them would make the couple lose respect for themselves, a breach of an unspoken contract that might even—who knows?—provoke immanent justice. Forcing themselves, obligating themselves, controlling themselves, holding themselves accountable—all of these things are part of their training for this new world. Destiny, weigher of souls and actions, is lenient only for those who deserve it.

These duties also help them to structure their time, keep them in the moment, fill up their minds, prevent them from dwelling too much on the future. Examining their own conscience and feeling proud of their accomplishments and efforts is what makes them human; it distinguishes them from the animals that are merely predators and keeps them at a slight distance from the caveman lifestyle that they sometimes feel they are living. If they are mimicking society, it means they still belong to it. The differences between their life here and their life in the fifteenth arrondissement should be only superficial.

THE WEATHER IS dismal and drizzly. Their anoraks, which were only intended to be worn for a short stroll, are now completely ripped up and no longer keep out the damp or the cold. Louise and Ludovic try to retrieve some wood planks for the fire from a shed by the water. The wood is spiky with old nails, and they have to concentrate so as not to hurt themselves. They work with their heads low and without saying a word. Every day the physical and mental fatigue weighs on them a little more.

At one point, Louise straightens up to massage her back, facing out to sea. At the mouth of the bay, an enormous ship, easily visible despite the mist, is sailing parallel to the coast. For a second, she thinks she's hallucinating. Then, as though a dam has given way in her chest, she feels a heat spreading through her, a lovely, sweet heat that makes her tremble.

"Lu . . . Ludo! Look!"

She feels petrified, doesn't even have the strength to hold out her arm, but she doesn't have to. He breaks into a nervous laugh.

"Ah! Quick, let's go to the dinghy!"

"No, wait, we should make a fire so that they see us. I'm going to go find gas."

All of a sudden they are feverish, frantic, the urgency pounding in their temples. They don't have time to think about the best strategy. When they had written their message with stones on the hills near the coast, it had seemed clear to them that a boat would pass close by, see the message, and cast anchor in the bay. But this boat is far away, probably too far to be able to distinguish anything other than a bit of land shrouded in mist. It's a huge ship, more than a hundred meters long—one of the cruise ships that brings tourists around Patagonia or Antarctica. Through the fog, the ship is awash in a thousand lights that highlight the locations of the decks, gangways, and cabins on its massive, dark silhouette. A pleasant, organized, easy, gentle world, right there, almost under their noses!

Several times on their trip, they had crossed paths with these floating cathedrals, and always mocked the old folks who were sipping their tea from behind bay windows while the two of them were out there living for real. But right now, they would give anything to be on the ship. They are seized with anxiety. What if the boat doesn't see them? Louise rushes toward their lodgings to find the lighter, while Ludovic dashes toward the beach and the dinghy. When Louise comes back out, she sees that they haven't understood each other.

"Ludo, stop! We have to make a fire!"

She joins him, her heart pounding. Where is the ship? It has passed the middle of the bay and is continuing calmly on its way. No! Stop! Stay! Shouting in the direction of the

boat, she dives into the dinghy to disconnect the fuel tank so
that she can use it for the fire. But Ludovic abruptly pushes
her backward, saying:

"Are you crazy? We have to go catch up to them!"

"You idiot, we'll never catch up, they're going too fast
and they won't see us. We have to make a fire . . ."

Before she can finish her sentence, he is on top of her,
shoving her away. In an instant, words and reason abandon
them. They are battling each other, possessed by raw rage,
their faces twisted up in anger and urgency. He is the stron-
ger of the two, but she is fighting back mercilessly, biting and
scratching. Their fused bodies and heavy breathing would
be reminiscent of a pair of lovers in the throes of passion if
it weren't for their eyes blazing with a sudden hatred. Their
lives are at stake.

Ludovic finally gets the upper hand and pushes her back
onto the sand, where she collapses, bleeding from her nose.
Taking advantage of the moment, Ludovic pushes the little
boat into the water with a grunt of triumph. He tries three
times, unsuccessfully, to start the motor; in his haste, he has
forgotten to open the fuel tank. His hands are trembling, and
he can feel his heart thumping in his chest so hard it hurts.
Time stands still. Finally, the outboard motor hiccups and
he speeds off at full throttle.

Louise, groggy, crawls along the sand, moaning.

"No! Oh, no! Come back. I need the gas . . ."

She slams her fist on the ground, sending a spray of sand
into the air. She is in unbearable distress, trembling from
the violence that had just broken out between the two of

them. If she had had a knife, she would have stabbed him in the back—stabbed the man whom she suddenly hates with every fiber of her being. Shame sweeps over her, but she doesn't know whether it's because she lost the fight or because she had lost control, letting her impulses and limbic system take over.

The sound of the outboard motor reinvigorates her. She leaps to her feet and, clutching the lighter tightly enough to shatter her knuckles, charges toward the pile of wood that they had been tearing down just a few minutes earlier. Ignoring the nails and splinters that are ripping up her hands, she collects the pieces that seem the smallest and the driest and tries to light them on fire. But it's a lost cause; all she manages to do is burn the tips of her fingers. She doesn't want to look out to sea. She has to keep concentrating. Maybe the cruise ship has slowed down so that its passengers can admire the landscape? Wildly, she looks around her. Some old newspapers have been nailed onto a plank, presumably in some semblance of insulation. She tears them down and lights them, trembling . . . oh God, please . . . She hasn't prayed since, at the age of eighteen, she announced to her mother that she didn't believe in God and would no longer be attending mass.

A miracle! The flame flickers and catches on some splinters of wood. She sighs with happiness. Very carefully she adds some more kindling. In a few minutes, a tiny fire is smoldering, its eye glowing red. A little longer and she'll be able to add the rotten wood, which will give off some nice smoke. She straightens up.

The bay is empty. No ship, no dinghy—nothing but fog and the pallid silhouettes of the icebergs.

She collapses onto a ground that is too cold to give off even the slightest odor and begins to howl. Her despair, her hatred of stupid Ludovic who has just spoiled everything, and the aftereffects of their brawl all burst forth in a convulsive torrent. She feels herself going crazy. On top of all this chaos, the solitude is crushing her, like a sledgehammer breaking all of her bones. She is going to die. Which would be better, anyway, than this slow agony. Who will really mourn for her if Ludovic disappears? Her parents, who had so strongly disapproved of this trip, calling it "idiotic when you've got a good career"?

Is she always going to be "the little one," not even worth paying attention to? Her scream soars out into the deserted bay, growing louder, then hoarser, turning into sobs and then back into a scream that is even more anguished than before. Two frightened penguins run away from her, wings flapping.

Ludovic, at full throttle, has reached the mouth of the bay. There he runs into a strong chop that hits the boat sideways, slowing it down. Somehow, he manages to stand up, take off his jacket, and wave it furiously above his head. The ship is getting farther away. Come on, there must be a sailor smoking outside, or a tourist who's more curious than the others. He remembers a story about a guy who had fallen into the Mediterranean and been saved by the cook, who was emptying food scraps and had miraculously spotted him. The boat is rocking in all directions, throwing him off-balance. He has to get to the ship—there's no other choice. He accelerates again, using one hand to bail out the water that's splashing inside the boat.

After half an hour, the cruise ship is nothing more than a glimmer dancing far off in the gray distance. It's inadmissible, it's intolerable—but it's the truth. He feels like a convict whose sentence has been inexplicably extended despite model behavior. Rage, frustration, and distress form a suffocating lump in his throat. They've been struggling for weeks, bravely enduring this pitiful existence. He's even tried to keep joking around to keep up Louise's morale, has gone along with the thousand ridiculous rituals that she instituted. All that for what? So that this damn boat could come taunt them! Is there no justice?

All of a sudden, he is overwhelmed by the desire for normal, simple things—the world of the cruise ship, with showers and soft music played at well-laid tables, and also further, beyond the horizon, the world of the people who right now are returning home, swearing when they get stuck in traffic, getting a drink with friends. He wants his couch and his computer. He wants the sound of his keys jangling when he takes them out of his pocket, the smell of a frying onion, even the smell of the metro when it rains. He wants . . .

A squall sends his wishes vanishing into the horizon. He is soaked and shivering, his head spinning. He imagines how he must look—bearded, emaciated, and in rags, on a rubber sausage bobbing on the waves—and is humiliated by his own weakness. When he finally decides to turn around, it's very late. Even at slow speed, he nearly capsizes several times. In order to keep the boat upright he has to follow the coast at an angle. Seen from a distance, the landscape is gloomy in shades of black and dirty white. Waves bare their teeth against a dark and desolate earth strewn with patches of snow. He stops the motor and lets the boat drift. What's the point of returning to such a hostile place? Wouldn't it be better to just be done with it? Night will fall, and cold will scoop him up in its indifferent claws; little by little, he will grow numb to it and fall asleep. He can stop fighting, put an end to this pointless nightmare. He can sleep—sleep without hunger, without the permanent anxiety about the next day. After weeks of battle, he suddenly feels so tired. The hope that was reawakened by the cruise ship has boomeranged back, devastating him. He is exhausted, incapable of movement, surrendered to the elements. Rolling himself into a ball at the back of the dinghy that's been battered by the swell, he lets his mind wander. He wants something gentle and warm, something or someone agreeable to help put him to sleep, make him disappear.

Let's see, who was the first girl he had kissed? Amélie? Yes. She wasn't very pretty, but the other boys had said that she wanted to. She had a protruding chin and a big nose, as did he. He remembers that when their faces drew closer to each other, he wondered how their appendages would fit together. Her saliva had been bland. He tries to find a more enjoyable memory. Louise. He had had to tame her, and this had filled him with pride. The first few times he entered her, he had felt her tense up, ready to flee. So he had drawn out the foreplay, caressing her, with sudden stops to stoke her desire, until one day she began to mewl like a little cat. Then her moans grew louder and higher in pitch until she was practically singing. That evening he felt as though he had understood all of femininity. He liked to put her on top of him, watch her small breasts spill forward like two triangles. His Louise, so little, his little Louise. He begins to croon:

"Little, little, so little . . ."

The boat is drifting like a dead fish. A giant petrel, intrigued, circles for a moment above him, but this huge thing doesn't look edible.

"Little, little . . ."

He is cold. Why isn't Louise coming to warm him up? She's mean. He's done so much for her! All he's asking for is a little warmth. Louise is a bad person, dry and hard, interested only in her damn mountains. If it weren't for him, she would have stayed an old maid, with her dusty taxes and her dumb climbing partners. He is so cold. He really needs someone to come warm him up. If not Louise, then his mama will come. Mama's so pretty. He loves it when she brings him to school, because then his friends can see her. But Mama isn't always nice, either, she's so busy. She has work . . .

"Not so much noise, Ludo, I'm coming from a meeting, I'm exhausted . . . Be good, pay attention, don't put your dirty hands on my dress . . . Be good, Irina is going to babysit you this evening, Mama is going out with Papa . . . Be good . . ."

Ludovic is always good. He curls up more tightly. The sea

spray is raining over his inert body, forming a pond in the bottom of the dinghy that oscillates as the boat rolls over each wave.

An angry murmur creeps into his head, breaking the thread of his bitter dream and preventing him from falling asleep. The sound of a waterfall, rhythmic and discordant, forces him to open his eyes. It is dusk, the interminable twilight of the Fifties. Slanted sunbeams collect under the clouds and cling to everything, gilding the streaks of green moss and highlighting the steep sides of the cliffs and long white trails of bird feces. Lower down, the waves are almost fluorescent as they boil and froth, crashing against the rock in high sprays and then sucking as they recede, leaving behind them long strands of water like jellyfish tentacles. He would like to close his eyes, drive away the unwelcome sight, but he can't, he can't anymore. The cliff that's several meters away, the one the wind is pushing him toward—that cliff means death. Immediate death, right there. He imagines his mangled body lying on the rocks, the protruding stones tearing his skin apart, the waves asphyxiating him. No! Not now, not here!

The little boat is entering the foamy breaker zone. He is tired, so tired, but he has to open his eyes. He crawls toward the motor. Pulling the starter rope takes all his energy. The sound of the ocean has gotten louder and louder, arousing in him such an intense fear that he feels reanimated by desperate strength. The motor starts, saving him from disaster at the last possible minute. In the growing darkness, he lets the boat follow the coast, the waves at his back.

He sails for a solid half hour, besieged by strange sensations. He feels limp, as though he has just come out of a long illness; his head is still spinning. He can no longer remember exactly what happened. All he can picture is the lights of the big ship, the last flickers of a fire that is about to go out. As night falls, he surprises himself by finding the whole episode funny. He's wandering around this unfamiliar coast all alone. He's free. If he weren't trembling like a malaria patient, he could imagine himself continuing on, like a kid dragging his feet in returning home, trying to scare himself for fun.

The cliff opens up in a thin indentation. It never gets completely dark at night in the Fifties at the end of the summer. There is still a pale thread of light on the horizon that allows him to see the black velvet carpet of smooth, protected water. He speeds toward it and, a few minutes later, the propeller knocks against the pebbles of a tiny beach. He jumps out of the boat and onto the ground, sits on the cold sand, and tries to remember what happened. Ah, that's it! It's coming back to him now. They saw the big ship and he pursued it, unsuccessfully. Why isn't Louise with him? His mind has erased the memory of their fight. He is soaked and all his limbs are trembling. He has to find her, whatever it takes. She must be nearly dead of fright to have been left alone. At least it wasn't him; solitude sends him into a panic.

At the bottom of a narrow valley, a stream tumbles down in the middle of a cliff that's almost completely smooth. Pulling the dinghy up onto the stones, he begins climbing up the stream, holding on to the slippery protrusions. The glacial water trickles onto his hands, paralyzing them. He feels like he is in a slow-motion film, hoisting himself up, sliding down, starting over again. Climbing over ledges and steeper sections, he finally makes it onto a plateau. The bad weather has passed by. There are still some jagged clouds, but they don't hide the moon, which is almost full and cerulean white. It makes the snowy areas look blindingly white and exaggerates the shadows. Every hill, every stone tooth, even the tiniest pebble looks bigger and eerier. He is haunted by images from films: *Nosferatu*, *Wuthering Heights*. The close-up shot of the moon masking the clouds signals that the hero's troubles are beginning. According to the script, he is supposed to be walking, walking through this pebbled desert. Somewhere, someone will shout: "Cut!"

The lights will turn on again, and someone will bring him a cup of steaming-hot tea and a blanket, telling him that he did well and that they'll be using the take. But of course nothing like that is happening, and he is still walking. He has only one thought left: Louise.

He does his best to follow the coastline. One hour? Two? Three? He knows only that he is cold, and that he sometimes wants to curl up on the ground, just for a moment, to warm up. But no: there is Louise. She is not going to be happy with him for being late for dinner. Suddenly, the plateau is interrupted by an ink-black carpet: the bay, their bay. On the other side, he can see, thanks to the light of the moon, the ruins of the whaling station. He imagines the thousands of nights that the ruins have been here, in the cold of the night—ignored, abandoned, sinking into decrepitude.

One hour? Two? Three? He climbs down carefully, feeling his way along, and wades through the ponds of the alluvial plain.

There it is, Number 40, the stairs, the door, the bed.

Louise screams as the vagrant with crazy eyes descends on her.

THE NEXT MORNING, they do not get up. The sun rises, and a ray of light briefly causes the dust to dance. It is deadly silent. They were so scared of losing each other that they had remained attached throughout the night. A light vapor rises from their fused bodies.

When she returned from the beach, Louise had gone directly to bed, incapable of doing anything else. After an hour or two, she forced herself to get up again and go back to the shore, which was growing dark. She was overcome by the same anguish that they had experienced upon realizing the *Jason* was gone, but this time it was Ludovic who was missing. Her worry obscured her memories of the fight and her anger. Hastily, she climbed the hill where they'd written their messages, but out at sea there was only the ocean, unrolling its gray-green carpet. Upon returning to Number 40, she went back to bed to ward off the cold. Keeping watch next to the fire would have seemed almost wrong in Ludovic's absence. She didn't even think of eating. He was somewhere out there, in the growing darkness. Of course, there was no way he had managed to catch up to the ship. Had he drowned? Was his skin already swelling up and going soft, becoming prey, flesh, an anonymous bit of meat? Was he somewhere along the coast? Wounded? Her powerlessness tormented her. The wait was infuriating. Finally, in half consciousness, she heard faltering footsteps on the stairs. He had returned.

Under the covers it is warm and damp from the clothes that they haven't taken off. All along their spines and up to their heads, they can feel the cold from outside, aggressive and repellent. Everything had happened so fast the day before. Their bodies and hearts are still exhausted. Time passes, or it doesn't; they don't know anymore. They each awaken from their torpor at different times and let themselves just fall back asleep. Everything outside is too cold, too difficult.

Louise finally wakes up for good with a start. She extricates herself from the bed. Her muscles are killing her, as though she had been beaten up. She needs air, the outside, to breathe freely. When she leaves the house, a biting little northerly wind offers her some relief. When she was climbing mountains, she had always loved the wind cutting across her face. She forces herself to walk, to start moving again. She paces up and down the beach, trying to clear her mind: one step, another, and another. The dried kelp crackles under her feet; little ripples in the ocean make hissing sounds; a seagull screeches. She lets these sounds wash over her. The intimate sounds of life going on, a life that now includes her. She concentrates on the sensations in the soles of her feet. Her shoes are falling apart, allowing her to feel what's on the ground: dry and soft sand, hard sand that's been smoothed out by the tide, stones, the swell of a shell. Heel, toe, heel, toe, she places her feet on the earth, a tiny little planet within the cosmos. The wind stings her hands: *Homo sapiens*, omnivorous mammal, warm-blooded. Yesterday the link that connected her to the normal world—the fifteenth arrondissement, city lights, heated apartments, running water—had broken. Thinking about it is painful, like a lost love, but if she doesn't grieve, there won't be space for anything else. Anything else? But what? She feels completely at the mercy of external events, just like the thin crustacean shell next to her that's getting tossed about by the wind. Bounce back! It's one of the catchphrases of our confused times—bouncing back after a divorce, or despite unemployment or sickness. The newspapers are full of examples of people who have an almost mystical faith in their own futures, modern phoenixes who reinvent their careers or houses or places in society. What she's experiencing must be similar to what foreigners feel when they are lost in European cities: incredulous despair, an unfixable sense of powerlessness.

She has never been suicidal. In fact, she has never even thought about it. Slicing open her veins with a rusty piece of metal? A cold rope around her neck? Just thinking about it makes her shiver, an instinctual reaction. Her pacing has dug a thin furrow in the sand. She is still there, still living; she has to keep going until the end.

When she returns to Number 40, she almost feels at ease again. The smell of cold smoke assaults her when she walks into the bedroom. Ludovic hasn't moved. He has pulled the blanket over his head so that the only thing visible is an inert bulge on the bed.

"Ludovic? Ludo? Sweetheart, can you hear me?"

She sits on the bed, pulls the blanket down, and takes his face in her hands. Tears have left distinct furrows on his dirty cheeks. They talk for a long time. At first it is just her monologuing, but little by little he ventures some mumbles, a few syllables. He doesn't believe in anything anymore. It's over, they're screwed, they're useless, they're going to die there, and it's just as well. Everything is his fault—the trip, the island, the walk, the cruise ship. He asks for forgiveness. She consoles him, forcing herself to be upbeat even though she doesn't really feel that way, refuting his arguments, encouraging him, inspiring him. Like a mother. She doesn't feel anger or pity or tenderness; she just wants him to get up so that she isn't left alone.

In the end, he is hungry.

For Louise, this is a new feeling. Until now, she has slipped into the cracks of other people's lives—her climbing partners, her colleagues, Ludovic. When you're "the little one," you give your opinion politely and only if it is asked for. Louise is sensible, so people like to ask for her opinion. She responds and that's all. She remembers the daydreams she'd had as a child. In the stories she told herself, she was the one in the lead role, the heroine. Sometimes she was admired, and sometimes people fought against her, but either way she was the main actress in her own life. Why had she given up on her dreams? When had she admitted that it was better not to become a mountaineering guide? What kind of cowardice had led her to renounce her ideals and content herself with a few hours per week leading a climbing team? In real life, she often thought of herself as incompetent, and preferred to let other people decide for her. But today she doesn't have the choice.

Ludovic, on the other hand, is dragging his feet. Something has broken deep inside of him. A sort of unruly pendulum is causing him to oscillate from optimism to pessimism, his moods as changeable as the clouds moving over the bay that sometimes let light in and other times block it out. One moment he imagines himself triumphant, returning to civilization after a Homeric challenge. The next moment all of it seems pointless. He's too worthless. If he could, he would stay huddled up under the dirty blankets. Stay there, daydream, escape through sleep, wait. Getting up is painful. The thought of returning to the grayish light, the damp, the thousands of bumps and scratches tormenting his weakened body is unbearable. He is beginning to hate their Number 40, the building they had put so much energy into fixing up. He can't even deal with its ridiculous name. Struggling, he gets up.

Louise understands. Seated on their whalebone stools in front of the stove, which thanks to her is roaring red-hot, they speak in low voices as though making a secret plan. She decides to go all in:

"We'll build a boat. Fix up the whaling ship that's in the shipyard. It's not in terrible shape."

"You're crazy. We're twenty-five hundred nautical miles from South Africa and eight hundred from the Falklands."

"So if we keep up an average of two knots every day, it's

feasible. The Falklands are against the wind, but we could get to South Africa in a month, or a month and a half. Remember Shackleton and how he crossed the Antarctic?"

"Okay, but we're not Shackleton. And what about food? Water?"

"Look, we'll take our time. We'll give ourselves the winter to fix up the boat and gather provisions. We have to save ourselves, Ludo."

Fired up, she describes the boat to him: its rounded flanks, the little cabin, a mast and sails cobbled together. It will be the *Jason 2*, their second chance.

He thinks about the very first time he saw her, in the TGV. Her eyes were sparkling with stars just as they are now. He hates the idea of having to decide anything. But she persists, trying hard to convince him. A good little soldier, charging into battle again. It's a pitiful sight. Thanks to mud stains, her jacket has long ceased to be light blue; her mop of hair is glued together with filth; her hands are scarred with gashes. She is arguing as much to reassure herself as she is to persuade Ludovic. Powerless, Ludovic gives in, with a bit of fascination for this skinny girl with endless energy. It's a relief to make a decision.

He remembers some religious images that his grandmother used to show him. A road that forked into two: the path to paradise was shrubland that thinned out a little at a time, while the route that seemed like the surer bet at first led to hell. Judeo-Christian nonsense? Sacrificial superstition? Who knows? At this point . . .

THE WHALING SHIP is lying on the shipyard platform like a sleeping monster. A fierce wind has pushed it around so much that it's smashed its own launching cradle. Almost a square meter of planking on the starboard side had given way when the boat collapsed. It is nine meters long and three across, and the fat hemp rope reinforced with rubber that still garnishes its flanks indicates that it must have been a pilot boat. It would have come up alongside fishing boats and guided them to the dock. Several planks are loose, and ribbons of wrinkly oakum are spilling out like handfuls of worms.

The thick oak has gone gray over the years and been covered with streaks of rust and bird droppings, but it still inspires confidence. On the deck, the cabin superstructure is completely open to the wind. In the manhole that served as a cockpit, all that remains of the wheel is a single rod gilded with rust. At the bow, other forms of life have claimed their territory. Fescue grass has sprouted in every crack, covering the prow with a coat of hay, and cormorants have taken over, knitting the grass into high nests. After scrutinizing the intruders worriedly with their royal-blue eyes set off by puffs of orange, the birds fly away reluctantly. Louise takes advantage of the opportunity to knock out a few chicks for their dinner. The inside of the ship is destroyed, filled with stagnant water. There's still a table and a bench solidly fastened down and some rickety cabinets, all of which are sticky with damp and blackened with fungi. What was once the motor is now just a rusty block.

Strangely, the monumental amount of work it will take to turn this wreck into a boat capable of crossing the southern seas reenergizes Ludovic, mitigating his feeling of failure. His enthusiasm is gone, but he's at least willing to sincerely devote himself to the task. The work is absorbing and he takes refuge in it. He is becoming an active participant in his own life again, no longer just an overwhelmed passive subject. Louise watches over him like a nurse accompanying her patient as he takes his first steps.

For a week they work on trying to hoist the boat upright so that they can remove the part that's destroyed. They drive in large wedges with a sledgehammer and prop the boat up with wooden beams that they've dragged over laboriously. Every millimeter that they get the boat off the ground is a victory, one step closer to freedom. Their DIY abilities are limited, to say the least. Normally whatever is broken just gets thrown out. Ludovic's experience is limited to a few treehouses and the maintenance on his bike; Louise has no experience whatsoever. Nailing planks over the hole is no easy feat. Every tool they need requires a few hours of work before they can use it. First they have to find it, and then they have to fix it up, scraping away at it, de-rusting, sharpening. And then they're not very good at using the tools— things slip, swerve, twist, break. Often the wood or iron ends up stained with their own blood. Their clumsiness bothers them. Arranging a couple of planks or hammering a nail in straight seems so simple, those types of things that you should just know how to do instinctually, like riding a bike. But now they're discovering the complexities, the unforeseen difficulties, the traps. Are they so useless?

The pioneers who were the heroes of the stories they read always seemed to deal with the problem in one go: "We built a cabin" or "With the remains of the ship, we made a rowboat."

Louise remembers how her father had built the closets in his shop himself to save money. It had all seemed very straightforward. When he was done, the shelves were straight, the doors closed, and the drawers pulled out smoothly. She realizes that neither she nor even her brothers would have been able to do even half of it. She and Ludovic have to fill in the hole, but they're incapable of cutting regular bevel joints to attach the planks together, so they decide instead to drive nails into the wood from the outside. With plane tools unearthed from the carpentry workshop, they clumsily fashion some laths to fit along the rounded edges of the planking. But the planks stick out at funny angles and the nails don't stay put, and the wood starts splitting under the strain. They finally end up using bolts, but the result is pathetic. The starboard hull is so swollen it looks like the cheek of someone with a tooth infection. It isn't watertight at all, and they have no idea how to caulk it. They have some vague memories of stories in which frigates were careened for this delicate operation and they are annoyed with themselves for not having paid more attention to the descriptions, which at the time had seemed overly detailed. The rudder also presents an insurmountable problem. The rusted fittings are fused together and it's so heavy there's no way they'll be able to move it.

They could have gotten discouraged. Under ordinary circumstances they would have abandoned the project a long time ago, letting more competent people take over for them. But working is a form of redemption. They've rediscovered the camaraderie that they had had while sailing. They're back to battling as a team, side by side. Back to cracking jokes. Timidly they start to make fun of themselves again, their clumsiness, their hopes. In the mornings they "go to work" like everyone else. In the evenings, surrounded by blond wood chips, with their backs on fire from having carried too much and their faces streaked with filth, they talk about their day and plan the next one. The semblance of a return to reality calms them down more than anything else and brings them together again. It's no longer a rare occurrence for one of them to slip their hands underneath the other's rags in the evening, for them to let themselves be carried away by each other's bodies, far from their damp shelter.

Their work in the shipyard advances slowly because they still need to search for food constantly.

Autumn takes over the island. In the mornings, cold nips at their faces and hands. As soon as they stop moving, they start shivering in their tattered clothing. It must be the beginning of March—the time that signaled a new beginning in their Parisian life, the time when they'd start planning their vacation. Here, the days are growing shorter and their surroundings are shrouded in gray. They don't have any choice other than to force themselves, day after day, whether it's raining or whether the wind is blowing, to seek out their meager rations and nourish the crazy hope about the whaling ship that is bringing them together.

One morning there is a torrential downpour. They agree to take a break, but in the early afternoon the weather gets even worse, and an intense storm shakes the base. The wind roars, wails, rages. The old sheet-metal structures seem to come to life, rumbling like drums calling and responding to one another as the gusts of wind advance. From time to time, a long cracking sound indicates that one of the structures has given in to the storm, ravaging the lost village a little more. They take shelter in Number 40, coughing a little from the smoke that the stove is blowing back at them. The rain is so dense that it forms a sheet in front of the window that's almost palpable. The world has disappeared, and their refuge is an island within an island, a fragment of a cloud they are floating inside.

They end up crawling into their bed, keeping one of their candles lit to ward off the dark as though they are children. When a particularly violent gust of wind strikes, the walls shake. For a moment they imagine the windows giving way and surrendering them, alone and naked, to the fury. They are seized by an animal fear—a cold, hard fear that overtakes them completely. At first they try to talk, murmuring

stories to each other from old times, when life was normal.
But this quickly becomes too much of an effort; they can
focus only on the racket outside. There they are, burrowing
like animals, fists clenched, flinching with each fit and start
of the wind. The day stretches on. They doze off, holding
hands. The little bit of light there was disappears; it must be
nighttime.

Ludovic, his head underneath the blanket, realizes that
tears are rolling down his cheeks without him really knowing why. He wonders if he will make it to the other side of
the storm alive. Escaping the island? They had been crazy
to think they could. If they'd been at sea in this weather,
their patched-up tub would have sunk without leaving even
a ring in the water. He feels like water is filling up his mouth
and his lungs, just like when he was in the dinghy after having chased the cruise ship.

Louise is also thinking about the whaling ship. Like
Ludovic, the fear of drowning is dancing before her eyes. She
decides that they have to stay on land. After all, here there
is life—water, plants, animals. They will adapt eventually.
She remembers stories about natives in Patagonia who lived
naked even in the cold of winter, hunting in the snow and
fishing in the ice. Apparently, they spoke affectionately about
their land, the same land that had so terrified the settlers.
Are she and Ludovic less skilled than those primitive people? Well, probably, because the benefits of their developed
civilization have cut them off from the age-old understanding of nature, the ancestral knowledge that allowed humans

to live on nothing. As they became civilized they had improved their lives' comfort and longevity; but their sophistication caused them to forget some of life's fundamentals, and now here they are, without any means of survival.

The next day is hardly any better. Once again, they spend the whole day underneath the blankets. Only Louise gets up to bring back a bit of dried penguin that they nibble at reluctantly. Finally, in the evening, the wind dies down, releasing its last breaths. At night there are only a few creaking sounds from the base, like the aftershocks of a tsunami.

The next day is calm, with a limpid sky that seems precarious. Instinctively they watch for signs that the tempest will return. Then, at last, they let out their breath.

In the shipyard, disaster awaits them. The weak braces they had used to prop up the ship have given way. The hull is once again lying on its side, sprawled on top of the planks that they had worked so hard to put in place, which have now burst.

They stand motionless, a few meters apart, and look at the annihilation of weeks of effort without any screams or tears. They no longer have the energy to experience any emotion. Both of them just feel empty, as dazed as a boxer stuck on the ropes, as stunned as they were on the day that the *Jason* disappeared. But this time, they had fought and they had lost.

The sight that awaits them in James Bay is even more distressing. The penguins have disappeared, leaving behind them a carpet of pinkish, smelly droppings. Louise and Ludovic had noticed before that the little ones were learn-

ing to swim, clumsily, and that the parents were goading
them on with pecks to force them to become independent.
Nature is not accommodating, and the birds have only a few
months to adjust. Cold is numbing the earth. Woe unto the
late bloomers and the weaklings, who can't reach the protection of the ocean in time. The storm has accelerated their
retreat. Out of the tens of thousands of birds, only a few
hundred are still wandering around the deserted battlefield.

For the next three days, tormented by urgency, Ludovic
and Louise try to save what they can, capturing as many
penguins as possible. They've gotten much more dexterous
in their routine. Stones no longer roll underneath their feet
when they hurtle down the hill, and they know how to an-
ticipate the animals' erratic attempts at escape, beating them
with their sticks with just the necessary amount of force
from their wrists and never missing their target. They load
themselves up with more and more animals to bring back to
Number 40. The nineteenth-century seal-hunters would have
gladly welcomed them into their community.

Their momentum comes to an abrupt halt with the arrival of snow on the fourth day. As soon as he opens his eyes,
Ludovic recognizes the blue-tinged light, the thick silence.
Just like when he was a child, he closes his eyes again to
savor the day to come. Snow isn't a particularly frequent occurrence in Antony. It quickly turns to a grayish slush that
sticks to the soles of your boots, but before that there is at
least one day when it is beautiful. He is going to open the
door and see a world made completely pure again, and he
will be its explorer. He remembers the moment of restraint

in front of the yard's blank page, the landscape that is both familiar and turned completely upside down. He remembers his eagerness to ruin the snow by rolling around in it, to take possession of it with peals of laughter, to leave his mark by sprawling on the ground and making snow angels.

But when they leave Number 40, they don't find any such joy. The snow has stopped falling, but the sky is still swollen with it, a uniform gray that absorbs the light. Dampness has blackened the wood and metal, which puncture the white blanket in every direction, making the ruins seem even more desolate. Other than a few three-toed seabird tracks, there is no sign of life. It gives Ludovic the impression of abandonment, of a deep sleep that precedes death—a far cry from feeling like the world has been made new. Louise isn't quite as morbid, but she is doing mental calculations. Winter is coming; in fact, winter is already here. There are only about forty dried-up penguins hanging in the kitchen, and the remains of the seal. What will they do after that?

Hand in hand, they go down to the beach. The snow after the storm signals a new phase in their life on the island. They are leaving behind them their disorderliness and untidiness, their instinctive ways of trying to stay alive. This white universe seems metaphorical: they are starting over from scratch. But this time they have nothing, neither food nor means of escape.

They don't speak. Slowly, they walk along the part of the beach that is closest to the water, where the snow stops suddenly. The weather is calm; the gray sea hisses softly on the sand; ribbons of clouds hang motionless about halfway up the cliffs; the sky presses down on them like the lid of a pot. They need a new story, an idea, some momentum to fill up this blank page. But it's fatigue that dominates, an irrepressible despondency that leaves them without strength or hope.

ACCORDING TO the records they've been keeping in their notebook, it's the end of April. The sun doesn't rise before midmorning. Their former regular activities—the morning gymnastics, the daily work schedule—are a thing of the past. Ever since the animals disappeared and the boat was crushed, they have felt like they're drifting, with no rules or constraints. Snow has been falling sporadically over the last fifteen days, and they've had to clear it away in order to access the stream, which is often covered with a thin film of ice.

The days weigh on them. They want to sleep—sleep to forget, sleep and then awaken miraculously saved from this nightmare that has lasted far too long.

They resolve to ration themselves to one penguin each per day. The best bits are fried in seal oil for lunch. They mix together the remains—shreds of flesh, broken bones, and even the skin, which they had refused to eat before—and simmer them for several hours. In the mornings and evenings, they make this soup and some hot water last as long as possible; it fills their stomachs, gives them a fleeting feeling of satiety. The rest of the time, hunger twists their insides, causes them to shiver and their heads to spin, provokes dizzy spells, and paralyzes all their movements, as though they are stuck and thrashing in a spiderweb. Hunger also gnaws at their minds, preventing them from thinking, making plans, even imagining the next day. Thanks to inactivity, they are stuck in a torpor. Their only occupations are cutting up planks to feed the stove and gathering a handful of shellfish at low tide, but even these things they are loath to do. The rest of the time they spend by the fire.

Ludovic has a cough that's getting deeper and deeper. He insists that it's just a sore throat, that it will pass, but Louise sees him instinctively putting his hand on his chest and suppressing a grimace. He has grown horribly thin, and all his joints protrude unhealthily under his skin. He walks with small steps, like an old man; any movement exhausts him. But despite everything, he is desperately trying to bring back his trademark optimism. He has carved dice and dominoes with scraps of wood and polished them carefully, mindful of both aesthetics and durability. It irritates Louise to see him absorbed in a useless task, but there's nothing else to do, so as long as he's occupied . . .

It annoys her even more that he is trying to play at normality.

"Another game?" he'll suggest. "I have to get revenge—you were too good last time. This time, I'll bet my bowl of soup for tonight."

"Stop being an idiot, look at you . . . You're nothing but skin and bones."

"Exactly, one bowl of hot water won't make a difference . . ."

Louise doesn't want to play. She doesn't want anything. Her time of being a good little soldier is over. She's not going to try anymore. She's done that her whole life and look at where it's gotten her—a total lost cause. Ludovic is driving her crazy with his false cheerfulness. She knows that she should pity him, try to make his life a little easier, since she's in better shape than he is, but she finds herself so indifferent it makes her feel guilty. From time to time she even feels raw hatred toward him, as uncontrollable as it is inexplicable. Scathing responses to his jokes are at the tip of her tongue, but she no longer wants to argue the way they used to.

She becomes obsessive and begins counting everything: the diminishing number of penguins, the number of shellfish they've collected, the number of pieces of wood they've added to the fire. Angrily, she realizes that her parents' shopkeeping mindset is alive and well in her. It is this genetic trait that exasperates her more than anything else. If time allows, she prefers to leave the house so that she doesn't have to see Ludovic coughing in the half-light and compulsively playing Yahtzee anymore.

The snow has made it impossible to access a good part of the base and the bottom of the valley, so she paces the beach instead. Frustrated, she counts her laps, unable to stop herself from doing so. Walking calms her, but it also makes her hungrier. She goes back inside.

"Baby, look, it's Christmas! I finally caught a rat."

Ludovic is holding the animal by the tail, its sliced throat still dripping blood. He's been trying different types of snares and traps for days, paying no mind to Louise's mocking. Eating a rat. She wants to blow him off, but her mouth is suddenly flooded with saliva. She is overwhelmed by the desire to feel the meat against the roof of her mouth, to crunch the little bones between her teeth.

IT'S IMPOSSIBLE to know what time it is—maybe the middle of the night. The silence is palpable. Louise isn't sleeping; she's tense, listening for the slightest creak or rustle to prove that she still belongs to the land of the living. The silence is a nonsound, like the nonexistence that they are living. It's like a nightmare in which everything has disappeared.

She's waking up like this more and more often, alerted by a silence that is anything but peaceful. Normally she wraps herself around Ludovic, who sleeps on his side; she spoons him, putting her hand on his chest and feeling the slow beating of his heart, and concentrates on listening to his breath— finally, a sound. In these moments she feels at peace with him, his large, abandoned body reawakening some emotion in her. It's more of a maternal feeling than a romantic one, but she wants to see his disarming smile spread across his face again. So she makes a whole bunch of resolutions for the next day: she'll be less curt, more tolerant. She knows that she won't stick to them.

Tonight, however, as she puts her arm around him, she is struck by a sudden feeling: she should flee! The idea comes to her as though it is self-evident, or worse, as though it has slowly been ripening in a part of her brain and is now imposing itself on her, taking advantage of her weakness. Thoughts unfold logically in her mind, without sentiment. They are just thoughts, each one leading to the next. They are going to die. Both of them. Winter has barely begun and already they have almost nothing left to eat. Ludovic is physically ill, but above all, his morale is completely gone. Its decline had started with the cruise ship episode, and then the collapse of the whaling ship finished it off. He has no more drive. Louise doesn't dare admit to herself that he is useless, but this general idea has already invaded her brain. The only solution left is for her to leave and to find the research station on her own. They had been cowardly not to have gone before. Now Ludovic is too weak for the trip. It's likely that he wouldn't survive it, either way. She can sense it, she knows it. She has to live. So she'll leave. That's it.

The next minute she is overcome with a feeling of infinite shame. She's going to leave without him? Wouldn't this mean abandoning him to his death? He is so weak. Is there nothing left of their love, or at the very least, a shred of compassion in her? Has she turned into an egoistic monster?

She thinks again of her childhood fantasies. When she was playing the heroine, she would never have abandoned the widow or the orphan. Quite the opposite: she would have dashed to someone else's aid, even if it endangered her own life. And yet here she is today, almost guilty of abandoning someone in danger. Not even a random person—the love of her life. Their relationship and their ease around each other aren't the only things undermined by deprivation and hardship. Fear has destroyed the most essential parts of herself: her feelings, her humanity. Here she is, stripped bare, obsessed with only her own survival, just like the other animals on the island.

Tears stream down her face. Ludovic is supposed to notice them. She wants him to turn around, put his arm around her, murmur just one word. Not even a caress: just one word, a grunt, to show her that he is still there, that he's not going to give up on anything, including himself. She concentrates hard on this idea, in the way that people do sometimes when they are hoping to influence their destiny through pure will.

But nothing happens. Ludovic doesn't move one millimeter. He could be dead. And if he dies, wouldn't he then be the one abandoning her? What would become of her then? She envisions herself even weaker than she is today, alone in this shack, as the fire slowly goes out and the rats' patrol comes closer and closer.

She breathes slowly to calm herself down. Take it easy, take it easy . . . It's just the worst time, the middle of the night, when both sky and soul are black—the time when everything unravels. Louise knows this time well; she has often fought against it. How many times has she woken up like this ever since she was a child, sure that she wouldn't know her lessons, that her mother would forget her birthday, that it would snow too much on the mountain, that Ludovic wouldn't call back? She forces herself to think that it is just her limbic system at work, her inner cavewoman seeing the fire go out in the middle of the night and doubting that the sun will come up the next morning.

She just has to manage to fall back asleep. She should soothe herself with a pleasant story, like you would do for a child. Go to sleep . . . sweet dreams, darling . . .

Rolling over, she nestles against Ludovic. Then she gags. He stinks. He smells like a vagrant, a trash can, like sweat and cold urine, like the old clothing that he no longer takes off, inside which his dirty body is stewing in its own juices. The smell suffocates her, even though she's never noticed it before. She must smell at least a bit better than this. She tries to clean herself up every evening. Ludovic could do the same as a courtesy to her. And there it is again, the refrain: he is not making any effort. Everything rests on her shoulders. She doesn't have the strength anymore to carry both of them, or the desire to share the meager food, or the willingness to put up with this smell of defeat. Smell doesn't lie, it's the most instinctive of the senses. You can lie with your gestures, or your words, or even the way you look at someone. But you can't lie when it comes to smell. Animals know this well—they make use of it, for better or for worse, when communicating their fear or their desire. Haven't humans tried to distance themselves from this fact for ages by covering themselves with perfumes, for this very reason?

Smell doesn't lie. And tonight, smell is telling her to flee immediately, to push Ludovic away.

In the most significant moments, Louise thinks, humans

are alone. Other people don't matter when you're facing life, death, major decisions. She should forget him and just live. It's her most fundamental of rights, her duty to herself.

The night is still just as black and calm. Only the red embers of the stove are smoldering. They never let the fire go out, and it is Louise's turn to watch over it. This means that Ludovic won't be startled out of his sleep when she gets up and starts rummaging around in the room. She collects her jacket and shoes and one of the sharpest knives, then hesitates a moment before grabbing the lighter and pocketing it. Groping around, she picks up the notebook, the pen, the ink, and a candle, which she lights before stoking the fire.

In the workshop, she scribbles:

"I'm going to look for help. I'll come back in a week at most."

She doesn't know if this promise is true. She'd like to believe it is, or at least pretend to believe it.

She hesitates, then adds:

"Take care of yourself. I love you."

At this exact moment she does not love him. She feels completely indifferent about him, in fact, but she does pity him. Her departure will be devastating. She's just throwing him a bone by writing this last sentence.

Already done thinking about Ludovic, she concentrates: a bottle to hold water, the backpack with the ice axes and the crampons . . . On the first floor, she takes down four of the hanging penguins, then thinks better of it and takes a fifth.

There are still fifteen left, so no one could accuse her of anything. But who would accuse her, anyway, and of what?

Outside, she is gripped by the cold. All she has to do is inhale and her nose freezes. For one second, she is tempted to return, to snuggle up to him. But come on—enough of this hesitation! She just needs to imagine that she's heading out on a mountaineering trip, with a beautiful route awaiting her.

There are a few cumulus clouds suspended in front of a half-moon that gives the snow a bluish tint. It's enough light for walking. There is no wind, and no sound coming from the old station, which looks like a movie set. Gloomy, like a Buffet painting. She has always hated that painter. Turning around quickly, she begins to make her way through the pure snow that comes up to her calves. She refuses to think of anything other than her route: go up the valley, veer off to the left, then look for a way across the first glacier, the one that produced the remarkable dry lake. After that, she doesn't really know. She remembers that the maps had shown a series of bays separated by other glaciers. Her destination must be in one of those bays, but which one? She concentrates on the faint crunch of the film of ice on top of the snow, followed by a hiss as her legs move through the softer snow underneath. The hypnotic sounds keep her from thinking, from reconsidering her impulsive decision. She collects a few pieces of wood to make a fire later, and a long stick with which to test the snow.

Her body is warming up. Her joints are functioning like

fine machinery. Just by putting one foot in front of the other, she is rediscovering old sensations; a life force floods her veins, and she feels immortal. Cautiously she makes her way up the valley, aware that one false step could be a catastrophe. She is alone, totally alone, and for some reason—she doesn't know why—that knowledge reassures and excites her.

The day is beginning to break, the light turning gray, when Louise allows herself to rest for the first time. She has made it without too much difficulty to the glacier, which will surely be her first real obstacle. The bay, which is still calm, is the color of wine. The base is barely visible under the snow. She doesn't want to think about Ludovic. She must not. He's probably waking up right now, maybe due to the cold, since the fire will have died down. He would be reaching over and feeling the empty space, already cold, where Louise should have been; he would call for her, jump to his feet, call out again, be seized with sudden anxiety. Louise can't stop herself from imagining it. He must still be groggy. She hopes that he'll get the fire going again right away. There must still be some embers—he'll be able to do it. He'll look for her, wondering why she had left so early, without telling him. He'll glance out the window: no, she isn't gathering shellfish on the shore. He'll leave the room, find her message. He'll run outside, calling her. By this point Louise realizes, confusedly, that she is telling herself the story she wants to believe. He'll come back inside, pensive, relieved that she hadn't asked for an opinion he wouldn't know how to give her and confident that she'll return soon.

He'll take down the skillet so that he can fry up his daily penguin.

It's not the time for daydreaming. She has to take advantage of every minute of the short day. Shaking her head, she fastens on her crampons and attacks the snow-covered slope.

HOW MANY TIMES has she thought she was going to die? How many times has she envisioned her ravaged corpse lying in whichever bizarre position it had landed in after falling, her clothing torn open and petrels picking at bits of her bare flesh? She's lost count, but it doesn't matter. Nothing matters now except the extreme concentration she has had to develop in order to put one foot in front of the other, to force her suffering body to move and keep moving.

She isn't counting the days: five, six, maybe seven. She doesn't know anymore how long it's been since she last ate, since she finished the last penguin. At first her stomach had burned with hunger and her head felt as heavy as an anvil, but then she felt light, as empty as the shells bouncing around on the shore. She has gone beyond hunger.

Her thoughts are few and murky. Her mind rambles, jumping from one memory to another, muddling together her teenage life, the storm drama, the day she met Ludovic. This is also due to a lack of sleep. The glacial cold has been torturing her since the very first night. At the highest altitudes of the island, the only way she can seek shelter is to bury herself in snow, huddled up and powerless as each of her limbs freezes in turn, until only a small warm pinprick remains deep inside her stomach. She has to force herself to

get up in the middle of the night, even if it's windy or snow-
ing, just so that she doesn't die. The last two nights, during
the storm, she hadn't slept at all. Keeping more or less in the
shelter of a cliff, she paced all night, sure that—like Monsieur Seguin's goat in the Daudet story—she would die before dawn. But then she didn't. She isn't dead. Now, she is
climbing slowly down a steep snowy slope, and at the bottom, barely visible through the fog and her own blurry vision, are two red roofs right next to the sea.

Of course nothing had gone according to her reckless plan.
Right away the glacier had proved itself diabolical. Under
pressure, the ice burst into a thousand bits and pieces, forming heaps of debris that were impossible to cross. So she
decided to go around it from above, struggling along the
bergschrund or in a jumble of crevasses that led her to a
dead end half the time. Sometimes she slipped into a fault,
plunging down a dark path between two cold, translucent
cliffs into the very heart of the glacier. When this happened,
she had to painstakingly carve out steps to extricate herself.
The first evening, she had managed to light a little fire directly on the rock, surrounded by ice that glinted red and
gold and seemed to come alive in the flickering flame. She
barely managed to cook her penguin, but the lukewarm flesh
proved itself comforting. It was the only time she was able
to light a fire.

The next day, the wind picked up and it rained. She spent
the whole day climbing up the glacier again, groping her
way along blindly. In the last of the daylight, a vast plateau
appeared. That's when she began to bury herself in the

snow—when there wasn't enough light to move forward. There was no chance of starting any kind of fire in this universe of ice, snow, and water. She gnawed at the raw flesh without even realizing that, a few weeks before, this half-putrefied meat would have caused her to vomit.

For days she wandered through the fog on the plateau. Without a compass, it was impossible to keep walking in a straight line. When the ghostly sun peeked through the fog, she tried to recalibrate herself, but she ended up only retracing her own steps. This was terrible but also reassuring, because the immaculate expanse of snow made her dizzy. No other human had ever walked there. This feeling, which would have been thrilling if she'd been on a mountaineering trip, sent her into an abyss of terror. Where were the people she so desperately needed? They seemed to have vanished for good. She was alone in the world. Later, looking back, she will not be able to explain how she didn't die of cold or hunger, or how she didn't get lost up there.

Now she is moving forward like a robot. Each step is a fight; the muscles in her legs are burning. She has to extricate her foot from the snow, transfer her weight carefully so that she doesn't sink down too deep, pull up the other leg, start over. Again and again. If it weren't for all her experience, and above all her hypnotic will to keep going, she would have collapsed by now. She is so exhausted by the end that she is counting fifteen steps, stopping to breathe, counting fifteen steps again. She accompanies herself by humming nursery rhymes, the ones that she remembers from when she was very young.

The sun has reappeared, making it easier to see. She has managed to reach the edge of a cliff and, far below, by some sort of miracle, she sees the roofs. She doesn't feel anything: she is beyond feeling, her mind as empty as her body. She just knows that she has to get to them.

THE DOOR IS BLOCKED by a large stone and a wooden bar suspended between two hooks. It creaks only a little upon opening. A vestibule contains a bench—clearly for removing one's shoes, given the boots lying underneath—across from a series of coat hooks and many worn oilskin jackets. The next door opens onto a vast wood-paneled room, a living-dining-kitchen area just like at home: there's a gas stove, a fridge, a sink, a long table, some chairs, and even two couches in front of a crate covered with magazines. Everything is decrepit and probably not too clean, but it's all there. The occupants had left their things everywhere, scattering the feathers, shells, and stones they'd found all over the furniture like children. Part of the wall is covered with photos that are blotchy with water damage—young people smiling in front of a good meal, or carrying a wounded bird or some indescribable piece of scientific equipment. She hasn't yet opened the loose shutters, through which a faint light filters in, causing shafts of dust to dance. All is silent. Louise moves forward and falls on her knees onto the floor. She has a strong urge to vomit, but she hasn't had anything in her stomach for a long time. She has no energy left, not even enough to get up. All of her limbs are trembling. She has succeeded; the nightmare is over.

With one last burst of energy, she opens the cupboards and practically inhales, at random, a handful of sugar, some raw pasta, granola bars. Finally she drags herself to the couch and falls onto it, half-asleep and half–passed out. She doesn't know how long she sleeps. During the night she wakes up and falls back asleep several times. When she wakes up for good, it's daytime.

Despite her hunger, this time she calmly takes each thing out of the cupboard; as she does she feels the cold smoothness of the dishes, the weight of the thick-bottomed casserole dish, the rattling of the spaghetti when she shakes its cardboard box. She forces herself to cook the pasta well and heat up the tomato sauce. Then she sets the table, her mouth watering. After wolfing down the food, she goes back to sleep, in a real bed this time. Adjoining the big room are two little ones that contain a dozen bunk beds with nicely arranged duvets. She falls immediately into a deep sleep, as though she's closing the door on the last several months.

For the first two days, she feels far too weak to risk the return trip. It's a struggle just to fetch water, and she hates doing it, feeling as though this long-sought haven could disappear with a wave of a magic wand during her absence. She sleeps a lot. She has taken inventory of the food supply at great length, feeling more awed than she has ever felt before, even at Christmas as a little girl. There's a little of everything—canned food, dried fruit, pasta, rice, dehydrated vegetables. She thinks she might die of pleasure when she eats half a peach, letting the syrupy juice slide down her throat. She licks the can of baked beans clean.

In a corner of her mind, she knows that Ludovic is still back there, but for the time being the distance seems impossible to cross. She does think of him when, slightly revived, she begins exploring her domain. She discovers what is supposed to pass for a bathroom—a cubbyhole with a bath and a sink that have to be filled by hand, with a bucket.

Above the fly-specked sink is a mirror that makes her flinch violently. That's her? With the plastered-down hair that makes her head look like a bird skull? The enormous eyes sunken into deep purple sockets? The red and blotchy skin covered in patches of blackish filth and frostbite? The face that looks like a corpse—yes, corpse, that's the word that comes to her. She realizes that she had been on the brink of giving out, of annihilation. She has to protect herself before going to anyone else's aid. She—Louise—must live. And then she'll see about anything else afterward. This reminds her of the security announcement they always make on planes, the one that always shocked her, about how you're supposed to put on your own oxygen mask before that of your child. Now she understands why this has to be the case.

If she returns to the old base, she will die. That is certain. Even supposing that she's able to find her way back, there isn't enough food there to last until the next summer. She can't bring back enough food, nor can she drag Ludovic to where she currently is. A primitive and animal egoism has taken over her brain, and she attempts to justify it. Would one animal sacrifice itself for another? No. In life you have to protect yourself, to take care of yourself before you take care of others. Altruism is for the affluent. At her current level of destitution, it's not a step backward to think about herself first. It's just a necessary rearrangement of priorities.

The truth is that Louise is simply scared. The idea of taking the risk of crossing the mountain again fills her with terror, and the idea of going back to the old base and Number 40—which symbolize only failure and death—is even worse. Just thinking about it is like a punch in the stomach that makes it hard to breathe. Nothing can counterbalance how she feels, not even the fate of the man who is most important to her.

Apparently, a badly injured person releases endorphins that neutralize their pain. Similarly, as the days go by, Louise's mind draws a curtain around memories of Ludovic without her even realizing what is happening, saving her from the torment of making the decision. Instinctively she thinks of him less and less, as though his image were dissolving in the ambient fog, just like how eventually you will forget the contours of a dead loved one's face.

THE DAYS PASS. Louise doesn't go out very much. Her domain for this period—a life between parentheses—is the couch, dragged right up next to the coal stove. She reads and rereads the same insipid magazines, still enjoying them immensely, and does the crosswords. She daydreams, listening to the rain thumping on the metal roof and savoring with pleasure the fact that she is dry.

She spends hours heating up water, filling the bath, and letting herself float in it, rousing herself from her semicoma only when the water gets cold. Her hair chopped off with scissors, her nails clipped, her body clothed in too-big but comfortable apparel, she fights half-heartedly against an urge to binge-eat that sends her to cook rice or pasta at all hours of the day and night. She's putting some weight back on. Ludovic is nothing but a shadow, a memory that's been walled off somewhere in the back of her mind.

Several days later, Louise emerges from her lethargy to go explore the other little house. At first, she hadn't bothered, having seen that it was just a laboratory. Nothing good to eat in there. But then her curiosity and her lack of anything else to do get the better of her, and she discovers a two-way radio. Communicating, being connected, talking to other people, calling for help—the thought of all of this gives her the chills. On the *Jason*, they hadn't had this type of device; they'd preferred a little satellite telephone. But she'd seen transceivers being operated out of the corner of her eye at several mountain huts that had used them because they were cheaper. First of all, she needs electricity, for which she will have to start the generator in the shed.

It takes her three days before she succeeds, mostly by luck. There isn't a lot of gas, but there's enough. This first victory over technology fills her with hope. It shouldn't be that hard to make the transmitter work. She turns dials and presses switches on and off at random. Numbers begin flashing on the display; the speaker whistles, growls, crackles. She wishes there were an instruction manual. Every now and then she does hear strange voices and becomes hopeful again, shouts

into the microphone. It's driving her crazy that, in the age of
the internet, she is so ignorant that she can't even figure out
how to make a radio work. Everything happens so fast these
days; a device that's not even twenty years old is already ob-
solete, or else no one knows how to use it anymore. Finally,
her fear of running out of gas comes true. She cries, overcome with the same feeling of powerlessness that she had
felt when the cruise ship disappeared into the mist. Then,
resigned, she decides that there's no use fighting it. These
false hopes are only destroying her morale. Better to wait
until help arrives on its own; the situation will resolve itself, for better or for worse. Right now, the worst no longer
scares her.

Louise waits. Comfortably, she waits. The days grow gray
outside the window. She has reinvented her own rituals. Waking up late, the taste of chocolate mixed with the sour taste
of powdered milk, flour fried and covered in jam, then hot
water so that she can wash up at length: these little plea-
sures take up a good part of the morning. Then she reads,
goes to look for coal, thinks about lunch, cooks, eats, takes a
nap, cleans up, and obsessively sorts through the contents of
the cabinets, and already it is almost nighttime. There's just
enough time to prepare another meal and eat it slowly while
looking out at the darkness invading the bay. She sleeps a
lot. There is easily enough coal and food for her to spend the
winter there by herself. The spring will come, and with it a
scientific research vessel. This whole episode will be behind
her. She has spun herself a cocoon that will keep her alive,

or rather that will keep her between two lives—the one before and the one after. She feels like a larva. There is nothing for her to do but wait to become a butterfly. She doesn't want to know what is happening at Number 40, doesn't even want to think about it. Here she is protected inside her fortress—her solitary fortress.

At least three weeks go by, maybe four. The island is in the worst part of winter, buried under meters of snow all the way up to the shore. Nothing moves other than some stray birds taking off. In the treeless landscape there is nothing for the wind to torture, so instead it rumbles in the corners of the house and sends the rain slapping against the window. The world is black-and-white, only a little greener by the sea, a little browner by the cliffs. There is a sense of eternity.

This morning, unusually, the clouds have parted and a liquid blue has taken over the sky. Louise is in the mood to take a walk. This nice weather has come just in time. She hasn't been sleeping as well for the past few nights. She'd like to chalk it up to the lack of exercise. In her dreams, something—or rather, someone—has been calling to her.

In the protected part of the bay, the water has frozen and the tide has deposited little pieces of ice that sparkle in the sun like armfuls of glass beads. Birds are pecking at it tirelessly. She wishes she could just be like them, wholly absorbed in daily life—eating, sleeping, surviving the winter. But lately she hasn't been able to surrender herself to routine anymore. Is it quiet remorse that's eating away at her? Memories come to her in flashes: his forearms constellated with freckles from the sun, the irises of his eyes turning green whenever he is annoyed, the strange throaty noise he makes after orgasm. The invigorating morning air is clearing away the cloak of fog in her head just as it clears away the sea mist. The faster she walks, the more images float to the surface of her consciousness. It's not the suffering and desperate man she is remembering, but the one whom she had loved and followed to the end of the earth—a joyful, energetic man whose arms she once again dreams of throwing herself into, a man whom she had almost managed to forget and who is now leaping back into her mind. Why now? Is it because she has physically recovered?

So now it is time for doubt, followed by suffering. She paces up and down the beach. Today she is dressed well. Her jacket doesn't have rips in it that let the wind in. Her thick-soled boots protect her from the sharp pebbles. She suddenly feels ashamed of being so comfortable, and then irritated about feeling ashamed. Without really knowing why, she begins to run. She'll tire herself out, exhaust her body in order to calm her mind, to be able to sleep calmly again. Then she stops short. In the past she had made fun of the people she saw trotting around the pathways in Parc Mont-souris. And now here she is, using her body in the same pointless way! This waste of energy seems obscene when there is someone dying of hunger so close by. Everything comes flooding back to her, putting a brutal end to her time of respite. She regrets her coma-like rest immensely; she knows that she won't have any peace any longer. Her days by the stove are over.

For ten more long days, Louise searches for ways out of her dilemma. Returning to the stinking lair where she might just find a corpse that's been gnawed away at by rats, confronting the consequences of her own desertion: what good would that do? The thought is horrifying. But then she hates herself whenever she opens a packet of rice or adds sugar to her coffee. How do soldiers do it during a war? Don't they save themselves first? All those acts of heroism written about in novels only end up causing several more deaths. Should you live alone or die together?

For ten more days she sleeps badly, her life no longer tranquil. For ten more days her disgust grows. And then one morning she feels like she doesn't have a choice anymore.

Everything is calm, just like when she had left. The old base is also asleep under a blanket of snow. Louise has the sense that she is returning home to a familiar place but also, at the same time, seeing with fresh eyes the burst-open tanks and blackened walls.

The trip back had taken only three days. She was aided by mild weather and her significantly improved physical condition. Once she'd made the decision to return, she could deploy the energy that her climbing partners had so admired, her sense of urgency increasing as she went.

There isn't the slightest ribbon of smoke, or any footprints in the snow. Once again, Louise has the desire to flee, but it's too late. Here is Number 40—the wooden door, the concrete stairs, the echoing sound of her own steps. She calls out softly, then a little louder. A rat scurries away. The bedroom door squeaks like it usually does. A powerful smell—a mix of damp, urine, and excrement—makes it hard for her to breathe. The gray light lays bare the pointlessness of the old papers serving as insulation and the filthiness of the rags that form a protective heap on top of the bed and the form at its center.

"Ludovic?"

Louise isn't expecting a response. But in the middle of

the oval shape barely sticking out from under the blanket, she sees two big open eyes blinking very slowly. This isn't Ludovic anymore. His gray skin has collapsed over his bones, causing the bridge of his nose to jut out so that he looks like a bird of prey. His tangled beard and plastered-down hair are flecked with white. The man in front of her is old. Not a single muscle in his face moves, there's not the hint of a smile, nor a single word spoken—just his eyelids closing.

Louise draws closer and calls out to him softly, her voice quavering:

"Ludovic? Ludo, can you hear me? It's me, Louise."

He is staring at her now, but still there is no movement and no expression, as though the person in front of her is merely a disinterested spectator.

Sinking to her knees in front of the bed, Louise touches his wasted face. Underneath the blankets, she can feel the pointed, bony contours of his body. She talks, cries, takes him into her arms. He responds no more than a rag doll would. If he had been dead, she could have dealt with that; she had already almost resigned herself to it. But this empty stare is devastating.

Lighting a fire, she heats up some powdered milk that she had brought back with her. She slips some between his lips and he swallows with difficulty, his Adam's apple seeming to rise only reluctantly. Some of the liquid dribbles out of his half-open mouth. She has the impression that she is filling up a motionless wineskin rather than giving a human being something to drink.

Overcoming the urge to retch, she tries to wash him. Each

of his joints protrudes from skin that sags like too-big clothing. His legs are covered with bruises, scabs, traces of excrement. What had happened? Did he attempt to venture out
into the mountains? Did he get hurt and come back here,
waiting desperately for her to return?

There is no other mattress, so she has to settle for sliding
rags underneath him to insulate him from the damp.

While she's carefully handling his body, she sees him turn
his eyes toward her and sigh. This makes her feel better.
Ludovic, her Ludo, is going to recover. She has brought back
enough dehydrated food to revive him. She's even prepared
to make the whole trip again to get more. He will understand. He has to understand. It wasn't her fault. She was so
weak, so tired.

The evening takes her by surprise. A ray of sunlight beams
out from the base of the clouds, tinting the bedroom pink.
She now hates everything they had so patiently accumulated.
Never again will she eat penguin or seal. By behaving like
animals, they had almost died like animals. The wild, un-
tamed nature that she had so fervently sought while climbing or at sea now seems like her enemy. How stupid it had
been to come here! They had paid for their sins and learned
a terrible lesson, but everything is going to be okay now.
Ludovic will recover, people will come looking for them, and
they'll go back to their normal life. For the first time in a
long time, she can imagine herself making love, becoming
pregnant.

She speaks to him loudly, like she's heard you're supposed
to do with people in comas to help them cling to life. By the

light of a candle, she tries once again to feed him, then fixes up some semblance of a mattress at the foot of the bed using old newspapers and curls up in her sailing jacket. She doesn't have the courage to sleep next to him. The bed that reeks of urine repulses her, and the cold, skinny body in it even more so.

She tells herself that he'll sleep better alone.

Several times in the night she is woken up by the cold. Ludovic sleeps on. From time to time he lets out a big sigh and she thinks that he must be dreaming.

The dawn doesn't take her by surprise. It lasts so long at these latitudes. The sun refuses to rise, then drags itself behind a cloud; the day stretches out in gray before consenting to diffuse a bluish light. Louise takes advantage of this by finally falling asleep. Is it another big sigh that wakes her up? She shakes herself alert. It's Ludovic—he must be hungry. But no, he isn't hungry. He will never be hungry again.

She has never had the opportunity to look death in the face. When her grandparents died, all she saw was their heavy oak coffins; it "wasn't a sight for children." But nonetheless she understands the steadiness of his stare right away. Ludovic is no longer, no longer anything at all, just a mass of cells that nothing will be able to bring back to life and that will slowly decompose, dissipate, disappear. At first Louise is almost fascinated. How is it possible? She hadn't seen or heard anything. She had been at his side, almost close enough to touch him, throughout the whole night. And somehow the unthinkable had slipped past her. For it really is unthinkable. Ludovic is dead. She says the sentence out loud, as though to convince herself of it. The sound claws through the silence for an instant, then seems to be absorbed by the walls, the snow, the ocean.

The thought comes to her that he might have waited and wished for her just long enough, and that it's her arrival that caused him to die. It's why he gave up fighting after seeing her one last time. How cruel that would be! No, he can't have done that to her!

She puts her hand on his shoulder, buried under the covers, and shakes it gently. Nothing happens. She doesn't feel the tears streaming down her face and dripping onto her neck, dampening her polar fleece.

She cries, emptying herself through her eyes, drowning her sorrow and the sense of powerlessness that has gripped her ever since this accursed cruise went wrong. Sitting on the muddy fabric on the ground, she lets go. The fight is over; life has lost, it's gone, and so is the constant tension and battle to find solutions to the impossible, to keep going with nothing, far from everything and everyone. Merciless nature proved itself the strongest, but should mercy ever be expected from natural elements? Here, animals live and die every day.

Louise weeps for being alone, for not having come back early enough, for no longer knowing what to do. After what seems like an endless amount of time, she has no more tears. All the water has flowed from her body, a river of dismay. All that remains are her swollen eyes and a bad migraine.

Ludovic's eyes are already glassy, or rather imperceptibly veiled. Something in his pupils is solidifying, closing the door that connects him to other beings.

Dazed, Louise stays for a while watching the rising white sun illuminate the room. The air is so cold that no dust dances in the rays, and then there is the silence—that of the snow outside and the form on the bed—that washes over her, submerging her completely.

Finally she gets up, collects the backpack that she hadn't had time to unpack yesterday, and leaves the room.

PART II

Here

"**M**EETING'S IN AN hour. You ready?"

The tall redhead has hoisted herself on top of the half partition in the open-plan office. She bursts out laughing.

"Oh man, you do not look so good! Did you go out last night or something?"

Pierre-Yves grunts. He knew that inviting friends over to watch the game on a Tuesday evening when there was an editorial meeting the next morning was not wise. Especially because when he left the office yesterday, he was definitely not "ready": he didn't yet have a subject to pitch at the meeting and then investigate over the next two weeks. An hour to find something isn't much, but still, he doesn't regret the time he'd spent last week researching internet addiction, conducting long interviews with young people who were completely immersed in the virtual world. It had fascinated him. He knows that when he's excited about a subject, his work is good—very good, even—and that's why he writes for a weekly publication that's still surviving, more or less, at a time when many other media outlets are going under.

L'Actu is a reputable news magazine, neither leftist nor conservative, that specializes in off-kilter perspectives and unexpected subjects—the reason it still has readers. Marion, the redhead, is the talented culture reporter who always manages to unearth a Malian writer or something that everyone will soon be talking about. He and Simon write about miscellaneous news and society, which isn't bad at all: one page of news every week and a long article every two weeks. Up until last night, he had thought about doing a profile of a former businessman who had ended up out on the streets and was now trying to start a business that would offer services to homeless people. But when he'd gotten the guy on the phone, Pierre-Yves was bored by the businessman's moralizing about hard work and tenacity. If it wasn't interesting to him, it wouldn't be interesting to his readers.

Marion's intervention had at least pulled him out of his hungover torpor. He shifts in his chair. Ultimately, he loves to work under pressure, to feel the adrenaline buzzing through his veins. He has sixty minutes to unearth *the* idea. For fifteen minutes he rereads the notes he had jotted down off the cuff during meetings in the hopes of finding something there. There's nothing, so then he starts browsing around news sites in English, which are often ahead of French ones in terms of information.

On Reuters, he strikes gold. It's from the column "Oddly Enough," which Pierre-Yves likes because it's full of weird stories, and was published that very morning:

Stanley, Falkland Islands:

The British Antarctic Survey research vessel Ernest Shackleton, *on assignment at Stromness Island, reports that they have discovered a woman of French nationality who was shipwrecked eight months ago. Her partner is reported to*

have died of hunger, while she survived by eating birds and
seals before finding and taking shelter in the research station.
She will be brought back to Stanley immediately to be heard
by the authorities.

A twenty-first-century female Robinson Crusoe! It seems promising: two dramas, the shipwreck and then the death of her partner, plus survival in a hostile environment. It could easily be total trash as a story, but it could also make for a beautiful profile examining destitution, solitude, the loss of social structures. It all depends, of course, on what this girl has to say. But he has to hurry and make sure he can get the exclusive story. It's a scoop in the making—he can feel it.

Pierre-Yves's blood is humming in his veins. Delicious.

With the time difference, it's too early to call anyone in Stanley. He glances at Wikipedia: Stromness is a mountainous English southern island, all of it a nature reserve. The only people who go there are researchers in the summer. Five to fifteen degrees Celsius in the summer, minus five to minus fifteen in the winter. It's known for its massive colonies of king penguins, *Aptenodytes patagonicus*. Then there are several stunning landscape photos: icebergs, colonies of birds stretching as far as the eye can see, snow-covered peaks . . . Perfect. The illustrations will be beautiful.

His first instinct is to call the Ministry of Foreign Affairs. They must be up-to-date on the situation. He had a good contact there, an officer, from when he'd written an article on French people who were working in oil in Siberia. The ministry refers him to the Missing Persons department:

"Yes, the Foreign Office did send us the information. Her name is Louise Flambart. Her parents, as well as those of her partner, Ludovic Delatreille, declared them missing at sea somewhere between Ushuaia and Cape Town. A maritime alert was sent out eight months ago. According to the note the English sent us, the ship's captain described her as being in a state of psychological shock but good physical health. The Stanley authorities want to take a deposition, but she will be repatriated as soon as possible at the ministry's expense."

The voice on the other end of the telephone sighs, then adds:

"No one has asked us about this yet, but I'm sure it won't be long now."

Pierre-Yves has to talk the guy into giving him the phone number for the *Ernest Shackleton*. Fortunately, he's a fan of *L'Actu*.

Time has run out. Pierre-Yves scribbles down some notes and hurries into the meeting room.

"**H**ELLO, LOUISE, how are you?"

Pierre-Yves knows that he has to proceed gently. The captain of the *Ernest Shackleton* kept telling him: "She's doing better, but she's still fragile. She doesn't talk much and cries a lot."

Pierre-Yves had emphatically insisted that he was from the Ministry of Foreign Affairs, as otherwise the captain probably wouldn't have let him talk to Louise.

"Who are you?"

Her voice is hesitant, husky, rather serious—halfway between the voice of a woman who's cried too much and that of a blues singer. It has a certain power to it, weary but determined. On Louise's Facebook page, Pierre-Yves had found several photos of her on her way back from mountaineering trips and eating meals with her friends. He's looking at them now, zoomed in, and can't seem to reconcile the images with the timbre of the voice speaking to him right now. With her delicate frame and little triangular face, it seems like she should speak in a piercing tone, almost a chirp.

"Pierre-Yves Tasdour. I heard about your story, it's amazing. You've been incredibly brave. I'm a journalist at *L'Actu*. I'd like to speak with you for a minute. Have you been on board the *Ernest Shackleton* for long?"

"Three days."

"Can you tell me what happened when they arrived?"

He knows how to do his job, how to gain the upper hand. Everyone likes talking about themselves. You can't give people too much time to think, otherwise it ruins the spontaneity that readers love.

"I saw them out the window one morning as I was drinking my coffee. The boat dropped anchor in the bay."

"You were drinking your coffee?" The tone of her voice hadn't changed at all as she'd said this. "So you went outside, called out to them?"

"No. Right afterward they got in a dinghy and came to the base."

For a second, Pierre-Yves is thrown off-balance. There she was, finally seeing her saviors after all those horrible months, and she just continued to drink her coffee! Is she making fun of him? Is she reciting a script that she's already rehearsed so that people will leave her alone? Or has she already gone totally nuts?

"You weren't impatient? They were about to save you!"

"I don't know. I was there, they would have found me either way."

EVER SINCE she had closed the door on Number 40 and returned to the refuge of the base, Louise has been overcome by a deep torpor. The hours that followed, whether night or day, barely mattered to her. She would become absorbed in the boiling water for the pasta, the bubbles getting bigger and bigger and then bursting with a gurgle. She watched the rain drip down the windows and seep in through the frame. When spring came, she became fascinated by the albatrosses' courtship dance. No matter what the weather was like, she would go outside, sit down on the damp grass, and watch the animals waddle around seriously. They would face each other, wings halfway lifted, and perform secret choreography, taking little steps, beating their wings rhythmically, twisting their necks, and touching their beaks together, all accompanied by plaintive calls and throaty noises. Their large bodies were imbued with the grace of seduction. Louise had read, a long time ago, that the couples reunite every year, recognizing each other through their unique dances. She couldn't have said whether these sights brought her joy or comfort or even just a spark of interest. She didn't have any feelings anymore. They were back in the cold room at Number 40. She could not, must not, think of the person who was left behind there. Her mind had gone numb, immobilized, even frozen, just like the island underneath the snow. Only her body moved, carrying out the tasks necessary for survival. She dug around in the cupboards to feed herself. During the day, she kept her eyes open. At night, she closed them and slept without dreaming.

When the boat arrived, she felt neither relief nor anxiety. She knew that it would arrive one day, and voilà, there it was.

————

AT FIRST, she tells her story over the phone the same way she had told it to the officers on the *Ernest Shackleton*—automatically, one word after another. The wall of indifference that she had built in order to survive won't come down in a day. She would prefer to simply erase the events of the last eight months and be left alone in her comfortable stupor. She doesn't see anything wrong with continuing to contemplate the ballets of the boiling water in the stockpot and the birds on the shore. But she has to answer the questions, if only so that they'll leave her in peace.

"My partner? Yes, he stayed at the whaling station. He died. I don't know exactly how. One morning he just wasn't alive anymore."

Of course, she doesn't remember the sedatives she was given so that she didn't have to see the long parcel wrapped in emergency blankets being brought on board. Nor did she see the traces of vomit on the jacket of the officer who had discovered the body—or at least what was still left after the rats had gnawed away at it.

The conversation with Pierre-Yves is stretching on too long, and it's beginning to reawaken Louise's mind. This guy is irritating her.

"But why do you want to know all these things? What does it matter to you?"

"I told you, I'm a journalist."

A wave of mistrust hits Louise, like the first shudder of an EEG.

"But I don't want people to talk about me. Leave me in peace."

Pierre-Yves is thoughtful. At first, he had conscientiously written down everything Louise had said, since you should never rely on a recording. But now he's just doodling geometric designs and looking at the photos on his screen. He has noticed her beautiful eyes, full of laughter at the time the photo was taken, and it's stirred up a well of compassion in him. That's a good sign, anyway. If he's feeling empathetic, he'll write a better article. In fact, he realizes, it's more than empathy; it's fascination. The serious, calm voice recounting these events as though none of it—the fear, the hunger, the death—mattered. Briefly, he wonders how he would be feeling if he were her. But now here she is, suddenly bristling.

"Listen, Louise. Your story's making a splash here, a big one."

Technically, as of right now, this is a lie. But he knows that it will soon be true.

"You are probably going to be hassled. Every media outlet will want an interview. It's going to be tough for you. I understand that you need to rest and to spend time with your family. I won't bother you anymore. If other journalists contact you, tell them to get in touch with me. Pierre-Yves Tasdour, from *L'Actu*. Will you remember?"

Ordinarily, there is no way that such an absurd proposition would work. But Louise says yes. She would say yes to anything. She's had enough of this, even if he does seem nice.

"I'll let you go, Louise. I'll come find you when you get back to France. Take care of yourself. Sending hugs."

Why had he added this last sentence? It was ridiculous.

Now all he has to do is dash into the office of the editor in chief, Dion, so that he'll cancel the idiotic feature about a real-estate scandal that was supposed to run, then catch a train to Grenoble to visit the parents of his heroine.

PIERRE-YVES HAD DOWNLOADED a photo of 23 rue Montenvert in Grenoble in advance. The expensive-looking, unstylish house hidden behind a large and precise hedge of cedar trees led him to imagine a slightly uptight bourgeois family. The reality is even more exaggerated. The father is potbellied, almost entirely bald, and surly, with huge bags underneath his eyes; the mother is a little mouse, self-effacing and well-groomed, without a wrinkle in her blouse. Physically, she is a carbon copy of her daughter. They are in the living room, with its polished furniture, doilies, and figurines all in their proper places, and Pierre-Yves has been settled in with a cup of milky tea. He hadn't dared ask for a beer; that could have seemed rude.

Of course, Louise's parents are happy, extremely happy, to have found their daughter. But emotion isn't displayed openly in this family. Is this where Louise learned to speak so tonelessly? Their hands never leave the armrests, their gazes shift from the window to the sideboard, and their voices are polite—exactly the tone that you might use when talking to a visitor you don't dare send away.

Pierre-Yves thinks of his own parents. They were part of a generation in which it was considered improper to bother other people with your personal problems. You were supposed to put up a front, be "dignified." Emotional outbursts were barely even okay within relationships.

Finally he's able to put his finger on the cause of the father's annoyance.

"She had a good job. Why did she feel the need to go sail away in search of adventure? I must say that Ludovic wasn't a very serious boy. He was nice, of course, but a little scatter-brained, if you know what I mean."

Pierre-Yves can figure out the rest. They had given her a good education and hoped that she would give up on this mountaineering insanity. She was old enough to have a child. But instead she'd chosen to take off. He and his wife were scared. They wouldn't have thought to notify the authorities of their daughter's disappearance, but Ludovic's parents had gotten in touch with them and taken charge of everything.

"Those poor people!"

The mother's voice chokes up a little.

Pierre-Yves decides not to take a photo of the parents pretending to talk to their daughter on the phone. They would be terrible actors. But he does take with him a few snaps of Louise as a child, and some others of her with Ludovic, just in case.

On the train back, he looks at the photos for a long time. He feels like he is hot on the trail and time is running out. This whole affair will make a big splash in France; it's got all the right ingredients. Normally, a major investigative piece would take him two to three weeks, but in this case it's going to be published on page one of the next edition. The editorial team has given him free rein. Louise won't tell him much more, not now nor over the phone. She is depressed. Anyone would be. He had been disappointed in her parents. And he fears that Ludovic's family would be crying too much to talk. He wants to understand—he must understand—how the smiling and anonymous couple in the photos in front of him had descended into hell. Other, less scrupulous journalists would have simply invented a story. But he clings to his credibility. He has always thought that a journalist's job was to expose truths, if not *the* truth.

He scrutinizes the figures in the photos:

Ludovic is strong, a good-looking guy, with dimples and a full lower lip that's a little pouty. His eyes are clear and blue. He looks like he's sure of himself. Successful.

His clothing and hair are always disheveled. Maybe a sign that he's so comfortable with other people that he knows he can break the rules a little?

His arms are often wide open, palms out . . . or else he's putting his arm around her, pulling her close to him, touching her. It seems like he's constantly in motion—maybe he's hyperactive? Or he's just a big teddy bear who needs to be hugged? Either way, he's confident in himself and in his life. Definitely a generous person.

A nonstop grin, an unlined face: he's never suffered.

Louise is much more rigid, less at ease in her body. In several photos she is sitting with her legs bent and her arms wrapped around her knees, chin on her hands—a defensive position. When Ludovic's arm is around her shoulders, her own arms dangle a little stiffly, as though she's embarrassed.

Her face is open and youthful, like Ludovic's. Big, pretty green eyes, with a hint of moonlight, or maybe melancholy, and a mouth that's often pinched just a little: is she frustrated about something? Scared of losing her handsome Apollo?

A little smaller than average. Scrawny? Not really.

He concentrates on the photos. No! She's muscular, and as a result her joints—her wrists, her ankles, her neck, her hips—seem all the more delicate in comparison. She is strong and fragile at the same time.

The two of them are looking at each other in every one of the photos. They are in love: Pierre-Yves is sure of it. He prides himself on being an expert in romantic gazes. He can tell when there's a spark of excitement, a sense of surprise and amazement, as though they are constantly rediscovering each other. He's sure that they're very satisfied in the bedroom.

Back in Paris, Pierre-Yves gets down to business, working so hard he has to ask Simon for help. They launch a real investigation, tracking down colleagues of the couple on the sidewalks in front of the tax center and Foyd & Partners; Phil and Sam, Louise's climbing partners; Ludovic's parents, of course, although Pierre-Yves had the tact to not press them too hard; a scientist who studies the southern and Antarctic French territories to describe the islands; a military doctor specializing in survival; a nutritionist; a psychologist who works in crisis situations; and three old friends from school, found on Facebook.

So he has the context, and he's covered the psychological side of things. But what he doesn't have is the most essential part, how the events played out—the damage to the ship, survival, Ludovic's death. He tries to call the *Ernest Shackleton* again, but the captain blows him off.

Finally the news is published in the English press, and the next day it crosses the Channel. The race has begun, but he's had a long head start. He invites his contact at the ministry to lunch under the pretext of wanting to hear about the process for handling French nationals in crisis throughout the world. Trendy bistro, good wine, nice ambience . . . and bingo: he learns that Louise is leaving the Falklands tomorrow for London. The consulate will look after her for the night, and then she'll leave for Paris on a plane the next day. This won't be a secret for long. Since the media has already begun talking about it, the Under Secretary of State for French Nationals Abroad plans to go welcome her at the airport in Paris. They have to send out a press release.

Pierre-Yves is playing big.

Will the press release mention the stopover in London? he asks. Could he be introduced to someone at the consulate so that he could meet Louise there?

The officer sitting across from him grimaces. That's not his job . . . If the news were to get out . . .

Between the mango carpaccio and the coffee, Pierre-Yves insists. No one will find out. He mentions casually that thanks to the officer's help, he has already talked to Louise. Then, in a flash of inspiration, he adds:

"Anyway, this story is fascinating to me. I want to write

much more than an article. I want to write a book with her. So, see, it's crucial that I meet her before she's swamped with requests. I need her to be authentic with me. If the press release just didn't mention the stopover in London . . ."

He has just made up the book idea, but the more that he talks about it, the more it seems like a pretty good one.

He succeeds in getting the officer to call the consulate. No emails—nothing in writing.

Back on the Eurostar, Pierre-Yves is already dreaming of bookstore front-window displays.

PUSHING OPEN THE DOOR of a pub called the Kentucky, Louise thinks to herself that the English have no taste whatsoever. The long bar covered in soccer trophies might be nice, but the rest is dreary. The booths are dimly lit, and the wallpaper printed with brown flowers bears gruesome tobacco stains from when people were allowed to smoke inside. The tables are made of imitation plywood, with booths of scuffed leatherette. Despite all this, the establishment gives off an air of scruffy, familial intimacy. These reflections make Louise smile inwardly. She must be coming back to life if she's noticing such things.

BETWEEN THE TIME of her rescue and her arrival in the Falklands, she had remained mentally lethargic. The crew on the *Ernest Shackleton* had initially fussed over her, but soon found themselves perplexed by their new passenger. Was there a chance she could totally lose it if they bothered her too much?

So they left her in peace, bringing her meals to her room and smiling and talking about the weather whenever they saw her on the gangway. They were all eager for the competent authorities to take her off their hands.

Disembarking at Stanley, in the Falklands, had been a shock for Louise. Neat little houses with gardens full of lupine flowers in bloom, sash windows with immaculate curtains—even here, at the edge of the world, the "English Way of Life" reigned supreme in all its comfort and restraint. After having dreamed for so long of this normality, she found it hard to appreciate. Everything seemed so restricted, so superficial. She had lost the codes.

She took refuge in the hotel, spending almost an hour in the shower, until the manager came knocking on her door to ask if there had been a water leak. A hot shower! The one on the *Ernest Shackleton* had barely worked. In this one she could let the water stream over her body, direct the jet over each and every one of her muscles. She felt like she was cleaning the inside of her body as well as the outside, draining away the torpor, the bad dreams, and the despair along with the warm water. She looked at her hands: the skin was becoming soft and pale, puffing up around the calluses and tiny cuts that she no longer noticed.

Her soul was getting soft, too. The walls of numbness that she had built up in her head in order to survive were all crumbling at the same time. At the manager's behest, she had finally gotten out of the shower. Wrapped up in her only towel in the steamy little bathroom, she realized suddenly that she was soon going to need to face everything. Life would begin again: work; friends, maybe; Number 40—the real one! Would it be possible? Would she have the strength?

She thought of Ludovic with dread. She remembered that the captain had told her that they'd taken care of him. She hadn't asked any more questions. Everything was coming back to her: the greenish light, the tattered blanket, and his eyes . . . above all, his eyes! The fixed stare, the shrinking pupils, the veil already descending over them. The man whom she had abandoned. This was the first time since she had been rescued that she'd said those words to herself. She should have never left him; she should have come back for him sooner. She had gambled her life against Ludovic's.

She shivered and spent a long time drying herself with the towel. Normal life might have brought hot water, but it had also brought many other, less pleasant realities.

THEN THERE WAS the whole episode with those stupid inspectors. The two squat, stubby men who were supposed to take her statement at the station had been exasperating. In a crime-free place where the only misdemeanors were occasional alcohol-induced damages, they were puffed up on their own so-called importance. They began the conversation with a half hour of lecturing: Louise and Ludovic had violated the law by going to the island. It was well within their rights to send the case to a prosecutor. If the shipwrecked couple had attacked protected species, like penguins and seals, in order to survive, then they would ask her to describe in detail all the "damage" that they had inflicted on the station.

"You must know, madame, that it is a historical monument."

Well, these guys are total idiots, she thought to herself.

When the conversation turned to Ludovic's death, she realized in a flash that she needed to simplify the story. They had been hungry and cold, and Ludovic had grown weaker and then gotten sick after his pursuit of the cruise ship. There was nothing she could do. End of story.

This seemed to satisfy the two Pandoras, who didn't particularly care exactly *how* the Frenchman died.

Relieved, Louise remembered that day that telling the whole truth wasn't always a good idea. Nothing would bring Ludovic back. She could avoid exposing the messier, more complicated parts of the story. Anyway, who would actually understand? Only those who had gnawed at penguin for months on end would know what it took to save your own skin.

SHE DOESN'T HAVE TO WAIT at the pub with her milky tea for long. A guy walks in wearing black jeans and a houndstooth jacket, a smile on his round face and eyes alert behind square glasses with green frames, and she knows it must be him. Only a Parisian journalist could look like that. He makes a beeline for her.

"Louise, I'm so happy to see you! How are you?"

Leaning his paunch against the table, he calls for a beer in excellent English.

She is just like he imagined—bony, and swimming in a mauve sweater that they must have given her in the Falklands. Her knuckles protrude from her hands and her enormous eyes seem to have swallowed up the rest of her face. Or at least that's the effect of the hollows in her cheeks. She no longer has that naive, almost childlike air. Pierre-Yves is stricken. The look in her eyes is the same as that of migrants he has interviewed, fresh off their makeshift boats— lost, and full of recent tragedy. Of course, she's not heading to a refugee camp, but still, she is like them; she has the fragility of someone who's been shunted between two worlds.

His mind races. Unlike those unfortunate people, who are easy to ignore, Louise is a white European woman— someone his readers can relate to. It's horrible to say, but undocumented immigrants form an indistinguishable mass. Louise, though, is unique.

Pierre-Yves realizes that he had barely listened to her response to his question.

"I'm doing fine, thank you. Or at least better. But everything is happening so fast . . . I feel a little lost."

Louise is scared. She is getting dangerously close to the point where she will need to pull herself together. Starting tomorrow she'll have decisions to make. She had talked to her parents on the phone for a long time when she was in the Falklands and turned down their invitation to come live with them. Number 40 would have probably been fine, but they had sublet it to friends when they'd left, and she didn't dare call them. And anyway, the thought of going back to that apartment without Ludovic fills her with anguish. The hotel feels like the best match for her transitory existence, even if its impersonality frightens her.

"I understand, I understand," says Pierre-Yves, catching up with the conversation. "Listen, I have a lot of questions for you. Hopefully I won't tire you out. But first I have to tell you a few things that might help you."

For once, he is being sincere. He finds himself wanting almost to mother her. His cynical friends at the magazine would joke that he's reacting like a silly old woman with a lost cat. But it's the opposite. He's genuinely touched by this fragile girl. He's going to help her. He'll become her mentor—she's seriously going to need one.

He lays it all out for her: the pack of journalists who will be waiting for her tomorrow with the Under Secretary of State, the countless requests, the interviews, the talk shows, the passersby who will recognize her in the street, the publishers, the film directors . . . She won't have a moment of peace. But he, on the other hand, understands that she will need some time to herself. No one can recover from such an ordeal in just a few days. He'll help her deal with the whole circus, maybe even find her a PR agent. He's thinking of Alice, an old acquaintance. She's a reliable woman in her fifties who has managed many athletes' public indiscretions. A woman with tact. She's amazing at handling crises.

Louise is reeling. She doesn't want anything, hasn't asked for anything—no talk shows, no PR agents. She just wants to be left alone. Maybe she could go to the mountains and go climbing, tire out her body in the hopes of getting some sleep, concentrate on a handhold, a vein of rock darkened by a trickle of water, the smell of chalk on her fingertips. She could calm herself down. But what Pierre-Yves is talking about is total turmoil.

"Look, Louise, you won't be able to disappear. Everyone

is waiting for you. Your experience is unique. Being left without anything, caveperson-style! How did you keep going? It must have been insane to have to fight every day! All of France is going to be fascinated."

This perspective is too much for Louise. Anxiety is roiling her stomach. So the nightmare will never end? Head in her hands, she begins to shake like a hunted animal. She doesn't want anyone to interrogate her. She will stay here, in London.

Pierre-Yves feels a flash of irritation. Only his fingers drumming on his empty beer glass betray him. He has to get a grip and continue to speak calmly. Clearly, she doesn't realize. She's still in a state of shock. Of course the requests might be aggressive, and the curiosity might border on creepy or shameless. But how could she escape it? Louise's life has become public. In a way, it's her duty to share her experience.

Given how distressed she is, Pierre-Yves doesn't try to talk to her about the financial payoff. Being a heroine can bring in a lot of money. Enough to live a nice, easy life in the mountains afterward, for as long as she wants. But for that she'll have to play the game, with no room for mistakes.

"Well, let's go. I'll take you to dinner somewhere else. This place is too ugly."

JAMIE'S KITCHEN IS the opposite of the Kentucky—a cozy restaurant decorated in shades of pastel, with walls of varnished wood. Pierre-Yves comes here every time he's in London. The waitress sports blue hair, gleaming teeth, and a constant smile. In one corner, a row of green plants helps to muffle the noise of the room, and Pierre-Yves has reserved this table on purpose. It was the right move. For the first time, Louise savors a sense of well-being. This is exactly what she had been dreaming of: eating a nice meal in the warmth, surrounded by other humans, free to act however she likes, to leave the table whenever she feels like it, to open the door and see other faces . . .

Pierre-Yves resumes their conversation, more carefully this time. He tells her about some of the events she has missed: a celebrity's much-talked-about wedding, a block-buster movie, the gossip from the latest Olympics. He had been too brutal earlier. Then, gently, he tries again:

"Don't worry. I'll stay with you. I'll take care of the requests, and you can choose to do only what you want to do. Right now, I want to hear your story, Louise. In fact, I have tons of questions."

Feeling calmer, Louise allows Pierre-Yves to conduct the interview. At that moment, if he had just let her talk, she would have told him the whole story, exactly how it happened. But he's in a hurry. He's already outlined the article in his head. During the hour-and-a-half-long dinner, he needs precise answers to precise questions so that he can write the eight pages he has promised to write. What he wants is the meat of the story to flesh out the skeleton he's already constructed, details to use as pull quotes to catch a reader's eye.

Usually he's a better listener, but right now he doesn't have much time, and he's afraid that Louise will fall apart before they can finish.

So he asks questions and she responds obediently:

"How did you feel when you discovered that the bay was empty? What kind of equipment was there in Number 40? What does penguin taste like? How do you hunt a seal? When did Ludovic get sick? What did he die of, in your opinion? How did you find the research station? What do you want to do in the future? . . ."

Louise answers. The questions seem a little stupid to her, but she doesn't see a way to get out of answering them. She stops frequently to savor her lamb curry and vegetable crumble. She would have preferred to focus only on the meat sliding over her palate, the granulated texture of the crumble, the condiments that taste sweet and spicy at the same time.

Little by little, she opens up, talking more freely. She had been afraid that summoning the memories would make the nightmare begin again, but in fact it has exactly the opposite effect. Telling the story means that she really is alive and well in a nice London restaurant with a guy who's listening attentively. She has finally triumphed.

Everything would be perfect if she didn't feel a tremor deep down every time Ludovic's name is mentioned. He isn't there to savor the lamb and the crumble. When she talks about him, she lowers her voice, as though she doesn't want anyone to hear her. She evades the subject as much as possible, and out of consideration Pierre-Yves doesn't press.

He hasn't asked her many questions about her trip to the

scientific base, which seems to him like a minor point. She doesn't tell him that she did it twice. In fact, she never mentions that strange and shameful interlude at all. She doesn't have the words to justify it, or even to talk about it. It's better that it stays down there on the deserted island, far from human ears.

Louise feels like she is in a room for giants. The bed could fit five, and the TV across from it is more than a meter wide. Next to the TV is a heavy desk that could easily be used for an eight-person meeting. Although if you wanted to have a meeting, you could also use the second room, which has another desk, another TV, and leather couches arranged around a gigantic low smoked-glass table. A bouquet of flowers that's just as disproportionately sized sits imposingly on the table next to a basket of fruit. On a letter-sized piece of cardstock, Pierre Ménégier, the general manager of the Hilton Concorde, has written:

Welcome, and best wishes for a speedy recovery.

For the first time in weeks, Louise laughs. All alone in the massive room, she allows herself some amusement at the incongruity of it all. It had started when she'd arrived in the hotel lobby and the bellhop had ceremoniously asked her whether she would like for him to carry her luggage to her room. She had given him the two bouquets she'd received at the airport and the plastic bag with the toiletries purchased in the Falklands, and he placed them on the dresser as though he were performing a holy sacrament. She heard a thud as the door closed behind him, leaving her in a padded silence. And she laughed.

She grabs the bottle of champagne from its bucket. Ordinarily it would never have even occurred to her to drink alone, but something compels her to open the bottle. Just so that she can hear the sound of the cork popping, fill up the glass, and pour its contents into the sink if she feels like it. The idea of wasting something! No longer having to count or ration out dwindling supplies, or worry about the next day . . . being back in the land of abundance.

The bathroom is the size of a bedroom. Louise empties all the bottles of bath salts that are lined up like little soldiers around the sink into the bath and sinks into fifty centimeters of bubbles that smell strongly of vanilla. The water is so hot that her skin turns lobster red. She doesn't think about anything, and nearly dozes off in the amniotic fluid.

She has to figure out how to get her head in order, and her life, too, but the only thoughts that surface are flashes of memories from the last few hours.

There was the guy in a suit who gave her a limp hug and some flowers; Pierre-Yves had whispered to her that he was the Under Secretary of State. The photographer asked her to smile, but without showing her teeth, since that wouldn't look good in a photo. A woman held out a piece of paper and a pen, and Louise didn't understand what she was supposed to do with it. Again, it was Pierre-Yves who whispers to her, *autograph* . . . Before her interview, the television was advertising dog food that looked more appetizing than what she'd been eating several weeks before. She faced the microphones; there were questions, more microphones, more questions. What surprised her the most was the endless applause when she stepped into the VIP lounge.

It feels like she's entered the land of a strange tribe whose customs are no longer comprehensible to her.

And yet it is the same world and the same human beings that she had left less than a year ago.

THE FAMILY LUNCH that was arranged for her had been a total fiasco. Her parents, her two brothers, and their wives were brought to a restaurant, with *L'Actu* picking up the bill. It was a large brasserie near the magazine's offices, noisy and bustling—exactly the opposite of what Louise needed. In the midst of uproar, with conversations all around them and servers coming and going, the family attempted to reconnect with each other. They had, of course, fallen into each other's arms in the VIP lounge, under the surveilling lens of the camera. But the Flambart family is divided. The parents would prefer for all this fuss to die down. They fear the neighbors' gossip, the questions from the butcher or baker. Louise's brothers, on the other hand, aren't as obsessed with discretion. They're relieved that their little sister, their "little one," is still alive, and also flattered by the sudden fame that has reflected onto them.

Louise would have loved for their reunion to be simple. Even after a long separation, people who love each other can pick up the conversation right where they had left off, thanks to affection and a tacit understanding. But for so long, there had been so few conversations between them, so little understanding. She can tell that it's strange for them for her, "the little one," to be the center of attention. It's as if they're going to ask her to explain herself, to apologize for being the cause of all this chaos.

The majority of their questions concern the shipwreck and their battle for survival on the island. She finds this humiliating. She'd like to also tell them about all the good parts of the trip, the wonderful months of traveling. One of her sisters-in-law keeps coming back to the worst parts. For a moment Louise imagines her boasting at the hairdresser's:

"Yeah, my little sister-in-law strangled birds with her bare hands and ate them raw . . . Can you believe it?!"

Louise can't tell if this is funny or demeaning, as though she's being put on display for everyone to gawk at. Is there nothing left of their relationship but blame and attempts to absorb some of her fame? But then she feels annoyed with herself for being so insensitive to their suffering. They hadn't asked for anything, or gotten any pleasure out of her trip— only anguish when she'd disappeared. Can she really criticize them for not understanding?

Her father delivers a final blow, saying:

"Anyway, I told you that this trip wasn't a good idea."

She wishes she could shout at him: But it was! Maybe it ended badly, but she had never experienced anything as rich and dense, or lived as fully, as she had during the trip. She could swear that that's what they're actually criticizing her for. But she knows that she'll never be able to make them understand. She has always been different, incomprehensible. Nothing has changed. Except that the version of herself today is no longer "little"; her ordeals have made her grow up. Her family hasn't noticed this yet, and she doesn't know how to tell them. Defeated, she bows her head, like a little girl.

When her mother asks her what she is going to do—if she can start working again right away, get back the apartment she had sublet—her responses are just barely polite. She doesn't know, and it doesn't matter.

At least one thing is now clear: she doesn't want her family involved in her life any longer.

L UCKILY, the afternoon calms her down. The famous Alice—a pretty woman with bleached-blond hair and stylishly unfussy clothes—has shown up. She's an extroverted ball of energy with an easy, contagious laugh. Treating Louise like an old friend, Alice seems to imply that this is all just for fun, and that they're the ones who will be calling the shots. She has already negotiated a free week at the Hilton Concorde.

"It'll be great, you'll see. You absolutely deserve it. Kookaï and Zara have agreed to give you some clothes. I thought they might be your style, and you'll need some things to wear. Tomorrow I'll see about getting a hairdresser, too. And would you like a massage? Or a Turkish bath? It's so relaxing!"

Louise surrenders. Without asking for anything, they are offering her everything, pampering and complimenting her. As she goes in and out of the dressing rooms, she hears Alice

negotiating with magazines and radio and television pro-
grams on the phone, and it worries her a little. Sometimes
the conversation is about money.

"Don't worry. I'll handle everything and I'll go with you
everywhere so that they don't drive you crazy. Get the little
bolero jacket, it looks good on you, but not the green sweater.
It makes you look awful."

Alice is laughing and flitting around, and everything
seems simple.

L OUISE FINALLY GETS OUT of the bath and wraps herself up
in a thick robe. She burrows into the double row of cushions arranged on the bed. This level of luxury far surpasses
anything she has ever known, not to mention the hellhole
that was the old base. It has a soothing effect on her.

An hour later, Louise, Alice, and Pierre-Yves hold a coun-
cil of war over dinner. They've sent for food to be brought up
to the room, and Louise learns how heavy silver cutlery is.

After the shopping excursion, Alice, who hasn't forgotten her business responsibilities, had prepared image rights
contracts for Louise to sign.

"We're going to make a ton of money. I have almost everyone in my pocket. The TV coverage tonight, the newspapers tomorrow, and then especially the eight pages in *L'Actu*
will up the ante."

Then she launches into a detailed recitation of all the media
she has her eye on. She explains the negotiations—the interviews that will be free and the interviews that will be

paid, and how much—in far too much detail. Then she outlines the quasi hierarchy of journalists, and what to expect from each: the number of pages, photos or no photos, live or prerecorded.

Pierre-Yves notices that Louise has started to smooth down the fabric of her chair's armrests, just like her mother had done when he'd gone to see her. The family tic must be triggered in moments of embarrassment, when they feel like their privacy is being violated.

"Louise, you're now a public figure," he says. "You may not want to be, but you are, so you should just accept it and try to find some advantages. I've been a journalist for fifteen years, and we don't hear of stories like yours very often."

Louise lifts her arm weakly in denial.

"I'll say it again: you can't do anything about it. The thing that's so compelling about your adventure is that anyone can imagine it happening to them. We're all scared of losing everything—of finding ourselves socially outcast, or unemployed, or victim to a terrorist or nuclear attack . . . anything. But you—you fought and you survived. It's inspirational! When you were little, weren't there people you admired who motivated you to grow and to be better? Well, now you're the one with this role. Don't disappoint everyone!"

Pierre-Yves has aimed well. Ever since the beginning his intuition has been correct. Appealing on some level to Louise's sense of reason and altruism is exactly the right thing to do. It gives her a moral purpose for telling her story, which helps to counteract the exhibitionist aspect.

"You'll see that they'll all ask you the same questions, so

you can prepare your responses in advance. The secret is that you have to be the one in control. Alice won't disagree with me. Later, for the book, the two of us can take the time to go into more depth. I'll admit that what happened to you is fascinating to me, too."

Alice takes her arm gently.

"I know exactly how these journalists operate. Even," she adds with a little throaty laugh, "those like Pierre-Yves. I can assure you that everything will be fine."

Right now, surrounded by her two allies, Louise feels much more at ease. Except that Pierre-Yves saying the word "survived" has made her think about something else. There is something she has to do. The idea is making its way through her head, revealing itself a bit at a time, like the photographic film in the developing tank in the high school photography club. At first you'd see only vague black blotches, but then the outlines would start to become apparent, and finally the details—the textures and shadows—until all of a sudden the whole image was there, a real-life scene set down on the paper. At last she is able to put words to the feeling that she has been carrying around with confusion ever since the research ship appeared in the bay. She has to call Ludovic's parents.

She has to talk to them, because she is the one who survived. But she's not quite sure what she'll be able to say.

"Breakfast service, madame!"

Louise, who had slept heavily after the champagne and two glasses of Chablis, is jolted awake by the knock on the door. For a second, she wonders where she is and what day it is. But then everything comes back to her and she hurries into her robe, already embarrassed about having to make the server wait.

Like yesterday, she finds the service ridiculously formal, but her mouth waters at the sight of the basket overflowing with mini pastries and crusty bread and the row of little pots of jam. Even for breakfast there is a gigantic embroidered napkin and an abundance of cutlery. Louise is beginning to understand that wealth goes hand in hand with grandeur, heaviness, and abundance.

"I was told to bring you the paper, too. Have a nice day, madame. We are proud to have you here."

The trolley is loaded with a pile of newspapers. Louise experiences a shock upon seeing that she is on the cover of almost every one of the dailies. All the photos, taken yesterday at the airport, are similar, showing her looking pathetic in the too-big mauve sweater. The neon lights of the airport accentuate her pastiness and the hollows in her cheeks. Her badly cut hair hangs down on either side of her face, making it look even longer. She would almost find it funny, but the headlines are disturbing: they're nothing but variations on SHE ESCAPED FROM HELL, THE SURVIVOR OF THE COLD, LOUISE FLAMBART: FACING DEATH. This is far too much! Of course, she had anticipated a bit of bombast, but this is beyond the pale. Apart from two articles that mostly stick to the facts, the majority of them greatly embellish the cold, hunger, solitude, and Ludovic's death. She may recognize the quotes attributed to her, but the context makes them seem all the more dramatic. With irritation, she notices that she's depicted as overwhelmed, powerless, and at the mercy of the elements, even if she had talked at just as much length about how they had taken stock of what they had and battled for their own survival.

The headline of the *L'Actu* piece stands out from the rest: SHE SURVIVED AT THE EDGE OF THE WORLD. It annoys Louise; she sees in it an undertone of suspicion, almost an accusation. Is it her fault if she's alive?

For a second, she wonders if Pierre-Yves has caught wind of her first trip to the research base. She doesn't remember having told anyone about it.

Seeing the cover of *L'Actu* makes her shiver. She recognizes the photo immediately. In it, she and Ludovic are hugging each other and smiling. A cord is still looped around one of her shoulders, and he is brandishing his fist proudly. It's from five years ago. She remembers the trip, an easy route on the Aiguille de la Glière, as if it were yesterday. It was the second or third time that she had brought him with her, and he'd done well. His face in the photo is still red with exertion and his curls plastered down with sweat. His T-shirt, which is a little too fitted, shows off his muscles. He looks gorgeous. He had just finished the climb, and she had congratulated him and slipped into his arms. It must have been Sam, her constant climbing partner, who took the photo. The shot is lightly blurred, showing how quickly they had run toward each other. They are so carefree, so alive, so bursting with affection that suddenly, grief seems to hit Louise in the face.

Ever since Ludovic's death, Louise had been stuck on the mental images she had of him from Number 40. She didn't miss that version of him. She had been too preoccupied with her own survival. It required all her energy, leaving no room for sentiment or affection. But now that she is physically safe, her heart and mind are reasserting themselves. Looking at the photo makes her tremble with desire. She wants him here, with his blue eyes, his full lips, his arms that sometimes squeeze her a little too hard, his insatiable lust. A sense of vast emptiness washes over her, starting from her chest and moving down to her stomach and between her legs. She feels useless, as though acid has eaten away at her insides, leaving behind only an empty shell. The last time that she had cried for Ludovic was at Number 40, when she was looking at his emaciated face. Those were tears of powerlessness and shame. But today she is in despair, a lover feeling sorry for her own loss.

The tea is growing cold, its surface now coated with a thin, silvery film. In the huge room, Louise's sobs slowly become fewer and farther between. She just wants to sleep, to collapse, to leave this all behind.

Almost an hour later, when Alice knocks on the door, she finds Louise still in her robe, her face haggard. Seeing the scattered newspapers and the breakfast that has barely been touched, Alice puts her arms around Louise's shoulders, as though she were calming an upset child.

"Stay strong, Louise. I can imagine how you must be feeling. I lost a brother, three years ago. He committed suicide."

For once Alice is without her usual smile, and her voice breaks a little as she smooths down Louise's hair mechanically.

"You never really recover, but you can go on. Believe me—life will find you again. You have to keep going, and make sure that you see people, and stay active."

As she speaks, Alice regains control of herself, and her voice goes back to normal.

"You've already shown how strong you can be. You'll be able to get through this grief, too. Come on, get dressed. We both have a long day ahead of us. Everything will be all right," she adds, like a mantra.

Louise lets Alice take control: cold water on her face, a steaming shower, hot tea, new clothes, a taxi . . .

"Here, I bought you a cell phone," Alice says. "Be careful not to give the number to any media, otherwise you'll never be left alone."

Louise hadn't anticipated that her return would be so difficult. Down on the island, she had been obsessed with the idea of coming back, eating, getting warm, seeing people again. Had her life before been this complicated? Had she simply forgotten, or idealized, what it was like to live in the world with other people? If she had been alone, she would have simply gone back into hibernation, like she had done at the scientific base. But here there is Alice, who is taking care of everything and who never lets Louise out of her sight. Alice, who had revealed her own weakness just now, and whom Louise wants to please. So she lets herself be told what to do, reassured by the exuberant and motherly woman.

THE DAYS ARE flying by. It's already been three weeks since they had applauded for her at Orly, and Louise feels like people haven't stopped clapping since. Alice is there, always, all the time, repeating over and over:

"Don't worry, don't worry."

Together they run from TV studio to radio studio, with stops at hotel bars to meet with print journalists. They have even gone as far as Geneva and Brussels. At first, Louise was just letting herself be dragged from one place to another; anything as long as they didn't leave her. But now, she has to admit that she's enjoying it a little bit. The TV recordings are especially fun. So many people for such an unimpressive result! But everyone is kind. They call her by her first name. She likes being left in the hands of the makeup artists. Before, she had barely even worn eyeshadow, but now she is delighted to be dolled up by other people. The women apply the cosmetics to her face with delicate strokes as though they're painting a picture, rifling around in their makeup cases for pencils and tubes of foundation. They always have something nice to say about how brave she is, or else they ask for her autograph, a request that no longer throws her off. There's a dressing room with her name on the door and baskets of sweets that she crams in her mouth as though she is still hungry. She jokes to Alice that it must be great to be an actress, and that she'd love to try it. Alice bursts out laughing, as usual, then says seriously:

"I mean, if you'd like to, it could be a good idea. I'll talk to two or three directors and see if you could give it a shot."

Alice is incredible. Nothing can stop her.

What Louise especially likes at the TV studios are the huge, dark backstage areas, where the people talking into their headsets seem like they're talking to themselves. It's a tightly choreographed ballet. Everyone waits until it's suddenly their turn to carry out some small task, and then everything comes together. She likes to stay there, behind the scenes, in the midst of all the puppeteers.

The next thing she knows, she's being pushed into the light.

"You're on."

She walks onto the set and everyone claps. They ask her the questions that had been agreed upon beforehand. Her answers are always the same. She had quickly identified the anecdotes and phrases that had the right effect, and she repeats those. As she recounts her adventure again and again, shaping the details just as she did with the stories she used to tell herself as a child, it takes on a legendary quality. At first she feels bad about calling so much attention to herself. Bit by bit, she loses the ability to distinguish the story from the reality. She hasn't exactly lied about anything; she's just embellished some things, omitted others. Alice was right— what matters is that the story is good. No one will ever be able to verify the details. And there are some things that would require too much explanation. How could she talk about the fight she and Ludovic had when the cruise ship passed by? What good would it do for her to say that she sometimes felt like she would commit murder just for an extra spoonful of disgusting stew? Who would care that she had gone to the research base twice? In the grand scheme of things, amid the tranquilizing futility, none of it matters.

THE EVENING AFTER their first day of doing the media rounds, Louise can't fall asleep despite her fatigue. As soon as she turns off the light, she is bothered by how silent the room is. Or maybe that's not why she's anxious—maybe it's the cell phone Alice gave her. Ever since she's had it in her possession, she's run out of excuses for why she can't call Ludovic's parents. She had been relieved not to see them at Orly. She can't possibly pay them a visit, but she has to at least give them a call. Hopefully that will be enough.

She had never understood why she always feels so awkward around them. They had welcomed her graciously, but with a hint of condescension, like many parents who are used to their offspring's parade of conquests. Even if they had grown warmer toward her over time, Louise had always gotten the feeling that in their minds, she was living on borrowed time. Before her there had been Charlotte, Fanny, Sandrine, and who knows who else. After her, Ludovic's parents probably figured, there would be others. Louise could sometimes tell, thanks to the tiniest of hesitations, that they were trying not to get her name wrong.

Nor had she ever admitted to herself that she was jealous. Yes, jealous, of Ludovic's cultured and modern parents. Whenever the two families shared a meal, Louise would be in agony. Her mother would dress too fussily, in a dress that looked like it was from the eighties, and her father would look ridiculous in a suit and tie. Meanwhile, Hélène, Ludovic's mother, would look gorgeous in black stretch pants and a simple T-shirt under a pink jacket, while Jef, his father, would casually sport an Eden Park rugby jersey. Instinctively Louise had always taken the side of her own parents, mentally reproaching Ludovic's for accentuating the differences between them.

Once again, she found herself in the role of "the little one," but in another way: the unsophisticated little girlfriend and then the unsophisticated little fiancée, the one who didn't know how to mix a cocktail or go sailing, the one whom they took to see a Jeff Koons exhibit to further her education. This was humiliating for her, even if her in-laws' attitude would never turn into a full-blown crisis. They were courteous, but at heart they didn't give a damn if it were Louise or some other girl.

When she and Ludovic had decided to go on their boat trip, Hélène and Jef had been in favor of the plan:

"What a great idea! Enjoy it now, while you're young. Hey, maybe we'll come meet up with you in South Africa. It's a wonderful country. We have such good memories from when we went to Kruger Park!"

Just like Ludovic, they believed that life was supposed to

be a party. Obviously Louise's parents had not ever vacationed in Kruger Park.

At the family lunch that had taken place after Louise's return, she had learned that Jef and Hélène were the first ones to worry. They were used to getting one or two emails a week and found it strange that Louise and Ludovic were no longer answering. So they had alerted all the possible authorities: the police; the Minister of Foreign Affairs; the maritime search and rescue service; the consulates of Argentina, Chile, and South Africa; sailing magazines; and websites for travelers. Then they had tracked down sailors who were often in the area and struck up an extensive correspondence with them. This led to them getting in touch with one of the best-known marine weather routers, who researched all the storms that had occurred between Ushuaia and Cape Town over the previous six months. But nothing. Their only son had simply vanished.

The table in Hélène and Jef's living room went from being used to serve fancy cocktails to looking like it belonged in military headquarters, loaded down with maps, messages, and pieces of paper covered with calculations of hypothetical drifts from ocean currents. Hélène had allegedly started drinking, according to Louise's mother, who spoke to Hélène on the phone regularly.

LOUISE KNOWS ALL of this. All day, in Alice's company, she has put off making the call: there's too much noise, not enough time, she doesn't want the taxi driver to overhear, she has to hurry and get dressed for dinner, and then, finally, it's too late. Now she is brooding, unable to sleep. Tomorrow she has to do it, right away. She can't avoid her responsibility any longer. It's a little like how it was better to finish your homework quickly as soon as you returned from school on Saturdays at noon, so that it wasn't hanging over your head the whole weekend. She has to talk to them and get it over with.

Hélène picks up on the first ring. Her voice is harder and more curt than Louise remembers.

"It's Louise."

"Oh, my little Louise. I saw that you were back."

It's already not going well. "My little," and then the veiled criticism about not having come forward earlier. But Louise will let it go. The woman has just lost her beloved son. No one can recover from that.

"Forgive me, Hélène, the last few days have been so crazy. But I haven't stopped thinking about you two."

This is true. She has been haunted by Ludovic's parents. Remorse for the part she hasn't told anyone about is gnawing away at her. She spent all night ruminating about it: to tell them or not?

"Tell me everything, Louise, please. We'll see you soon for the burial, but I want to know right away."

The burial! Of course—they'd told her in the Falklands that the body had been recovered and would be repatriated. She hadn't allowed herself to think about it. The body . . .

the rats . . . She's overcome with a furious desire to vomit.
She murmurs:

"They're going to bring him back?"

"Yes. I don't know when, it seems to be very complicated,
but they'll do it. They absolutely must."

Hélène speaks with tragic determination.

And so Louise talks—about the accident, the fight for their
lives. And she lies. It's by omission, but she lies about that
damn trip to the scientific base. At any rate, the truth will
not bring Ludovic back, and it will make Hélène feel even
worse to think that there might have been an alternative.
The night when Louise made the decision to leave, she had
known that he was almost dead, broken inside. But that's not
something a mother would be able to hear.

The conversation lasts forty-five minutes, punctuated by
sobs from both sides of the phone. They are crying for Ludovic,
for their own pain, for the end of a type of innocence.

Louise finally hangs up, assuring Hélène that of course
she would like to know the date of the funeral as soon as
possible.

But in fact there's nothing in the world she'd like to
avoid more.

THE PROCESS OF reorganizing her life hits Louise just as hard. She had never paid attention to the everyday complexity of existence before. As she had come back from the Falklands without anything other than the pathetic little bag of toiletries, she has to get new papers and a new debit card, and buy another computer and cell phone for herself. Then she has to deal with her insurance company for the boat, who are refusing to pay on the grounds that she and Ludovic had been shipwrecked near an island that was off-limits. So she runs around meeting with various administrative officials and bankers, aided by her sudden fame, which softens them up. The friends who had been staying in her apartment offered to leave right away, but she refused. The thought of returning to the scene of her happy life scares her. After the week at the Hilton, she has moved into a midrange hotel in Montrouge. She hasn't yet managed to make up her mind to search for an apartment, like she had done when she was single.

The tax center in the fifteenth arrondissement rolled out the red carpet for her welcome-back ceremony. The director gave a warm speech, and her colleagues cheered and presented her with a "return to Parisian life" kit: a purse, hat, gloves, and umbrella. On the administrative side of things, her sabbatical year has expired, which means that theoretically, she's been crossed off the personnel list; however, they have promised her that they've already put in a request with the leadership team for an exception. Louise isn't totally sure that this will actually succeed, and anyway, just like with her old apartment, she doesn't really want to return to her old job. Just the thought of leaving the center in the evening and not going back to Number 40, not waiting for the jangle of Ludovic's keys in the lock, not grabbing her bag and going out for a romantic dinner, gives her the feeling of unbearable emptiness that she had first experienced that first morning at the Hilton, and which has been tormenting her regularly ever since.

The only unpleasant part is the summons to the police station in the fifteenth.

"We're sorry, madame, but we must take your deposition. There was a death, you see . . ."

It seems like half the officers of the station manage to pass by, and the hearing is completely incoherent. The chief of police, who had taken on the case himself, whispers her answers as he's asking the questions, and every two seconds he offers her a coffee. Louise can't really remember what she signed. She tore up her deposition as she left.

When she's not making the media rounds with Alice, she's with Pierre-Yves. They shut themselves up in her hotel room—distinctly smaller than that of the Hilton—and have coffees and mineral waters sent up. She sits on the bed, propped up against a pillow, hugging her bent knees as usual. He sits in the only chair, which he has turned to face her, and scratches in a graph-ruled notebook. The real work-horse is the tape recorder, an old Sony PCM that he's been lugging around for years. The terms that he negotiated with the publisher allow him to pay a student to transcribe the recordings. Pierre-Yves writes down only what comes to mind while Louise talks: questions to prod her with, illustrations or references to track down, people to contact, and above all, themes he can structure the book around. He doesn't want it to just be an adventure story. All along, he's been sure that Louise and Ludovic's story will resonate with every reader. She's holding up a mirror to their society, which may be sophisticated but in which everyone still risks losing status or wealth. Her story also echoes the theories about going back to nature, whether by choice or by force, that are becoming popular. On the first page of his note-book, he has written down the strongest elements:

- Suddenly being alone.
- Going from a society with everything to one that has nothing.
- Isolation at a time of global communication.
- Facing a hostile natural environment.
- Relearning the ways of our ancestors.

When he tries to put himself in their shoes, these things are what would have been the most difficult for him. He and Louise have spent several sessions talking about her child-hood, her education, and the way she was raised. Then they talked about why she and Ludovic had gone on the trip, how they'd prepared for it, how it all unfolded. He doesn't yet know if he'll include all of this in the book, but he needs to know so that he can better understand his characters.

But most of all, Pierre-Yves wants to crack the relationship between these two lost souls. Having quickly read up on shipwrecks, he understands that the real challenge is often the group's state of mind, the hierarchies and alliances that are formed. How the protagonists reveal themselves to be angels or demons, those who break down psychologically, far from any kind of social structure. That's the territory he wants to explore with her.

What truly fascinates Pierre-Yves is the fact that many people share the dream that Louise and Ludovic had: escaping their oppressive, stressful society and polluted cities and heading for the open sea, rediscovering nature, freedom, real human connection. And yet right before their eyes, this utopia had turned into a nightmare. He wants to understand. Was it their fault? Had they brought it upon themselves, or did they have no chance to begin with, given where they'd come from? Did living in a society of abundance cut them off completely from crucial reflexes?

He briefly considers getting dumped on a deserted island for a little while, just to see what it would be like. But the suffering woman in front of him is reason enough to decide against it.

For Louise, pouring out her story turns out to be therapeutic. For the first time in her life, she is the center of attention, the main attraction instead of an afterthought. Up until now, Ludovic had been the only one to have paid her so much attention. The media exposure is positive but superficial. But here, facing Pierre-Yves in the confinement of this austere room that resembles a psychologist's office, she feels like she truly exists. Her life unfolds and is put into perspective. She may not have found the meaning of her adventure, but at least she's able to lay out the pieces of the puzzle that brought her here and start to put them together.

Pierre-Yves, waiting attentively, takes note of any subjects that cause her tone of voice to change, like it had that first day when he spoke to her over the phone on the *Ernest Shackleton*. They're all sensitive subjects that he'd like to return to later. He doesn't want to rush her, and he especially doesn't want to hurt her. She's suffered enough as it is.

A little cynically, he had wondered whether they would end up in a relationship. At times he feels moved, looking at her—fragile, curled up on the bed, her green eyes vague and a ray of November sunlight highlighting the contrast between her pale skin and black bangs. But no. He feels more like her older brother. Any desire he has to take her into his arms is just so that he can console her for the loss of Ludovic, which he feels to be irreparable, and to protect her from the harsh world that might very well discard her as soon as she's grown tired of prime-time TV. A painter who's in love with his model would want to glorify her, but he, Pierre-Yves, just wants to analyze Louise, to put her eight-month-long catastrophe under a microscope in the hopes of extracting some sacred truth.

Louise doesn't have any problem talking to him about

the fight that she and Ludovic had when the cruise ship passed by, nor any of the other little disagreements. She also tells him about what they had shared—emotions, solidarity, complicity—which balances things out. All in all their relationship had been entirely normal, with good parts and bad parts, and for the most part it stayed that way. The only part that she still cannot bring up is that first trip to the research base. Pierre-Yves had sensed that she was holding something back when he noticed her wringing her hands in an unusual way as she explained her departure after Ludovic's death. But then he chalked this up to how difficult it was for her to think about her partner's agony. Her story is completely plausible: it would have been unthinkable for her to stay on at Number 40 afterward, so she left on an adventure that was maybe a tiny bit suicidal, then found the research base by chance. So why had he written down in his notebook that they would have to talk about that trip again?

Louise doesn't know exactly why she's keeping the whole thing secret, even from Pierre-Yves, whom she trusts completely. Whenever she tries to think about it, she feels an overwhelming sense of shame that seems to paralyze her brain. She would have to admit that she had betrayed her love, betrayed her righteous childhood dreams, betrayed even her own humanity. The more she talks without saying anything about that time, the more impossible it becomes for her to ever break her silence. Revealing her secret now would be disastrous. Ever since she came back, she's been relying on her image and on public sympathy to help her restart her life. Being treated like a heroine opens many doors, but a heroine isn't allowed to make mistakes. She has to be pure, perfect, unimpeachable. Even if she only changed that one part of her story, it would call the rest into question, sow doubt.

At times, after recounting a truncated version over and over, she finds herself in denial. How had it all actually happened? Did she really stay at the research station that long before going back to Number 40? After all, she hadn't counted the days. And hadn't Ludovic probably done some careless things himself, judging by the bruises on his legs? Couldn't it have been his own fault?

Often, when she and Pierre-Yves feel like they have done enough work, they go out arm in arm to get a drink at the bar downstairs. The noise of the coffee machines and saucers being stacked, the fogged-over windows that soften the view of the urban landscape, the smell of wet coats: Louise gets a glimpse of a life she'd like to live. Sitting across from each other, beers in front of them, they look like any other couple meeting up after the end of the workday.

That's what Louise would like: to become ordinary again. But a heroine isn't ordinary.

HÉLÈNE FINALLY CALLS. Louise had been beginning to hope that she never would. That Ludovic would stay in the Falklands, in the little cemetery full of gillyflowers that she had seen. But no, all the administrative complications had been worked out.

"The burial will be Thursday. We'll meet at the house at ten a.m. I've sent you the list of guests I thought of and whose addresses I have. With one thing and another, we'll be close to a hundred people, but if you see anyone that I've missed, add them. I didn't know all of your friends."

Hélène's voice is expressionless. She sounds as though she couldn't care less about whom Louise wants to invite. It's her son who's being buried, not Louise's partner. At any rate, Louise has no desire to get involved.

It is beautiful at the cemetery. The early-winter white light makes the granite gravestones gleam. Louise realizes that it feels nice to be outside. She's been avoiding anything evocative of nature ever since her return, refusing even Pierre-Yves's suggestions to take a walk in Parc Montsouris. When she isn't with him or Alice, she stays in her room, sprawled out in front of the television. She doesn't want to feel wind or rain, and especially not the cold, ever again.

They are all there—close friends and distant acquaintances; old school classmates who introduce themselves because she doesn't even know them; a gaggle of exes; Phil, Benoît, and Sam, just arrived that morning from the Alps; both families; Pierre-Yves; Alice . . . The atmosphere, livened up by the sun, is somewhere between that of a burial, a fashionable event, and a reunion of old friends. People are wiping away tears and hugging each other tightly, but also exclaiming at the sight of someone or other and already laughing about old memories.

When Louise sees the coffin, she almost faints. Only she can imagine what's inside. It must be a heap of mush and scraps, a far cry from the athletic body everyone remembers. She suddenly remembers the rat episode, after they'd gone to find penguins in James Bay, and flinches as though a rat were about to dart out of the coffin, its fur damp with blood and mucus. The coffin had been sealed before it was shipped internationally; not even Jef and Hélène were allowed to open it.

As Ludovic is being lowered into the ground, Louise is surprised to find herself thinking with relief: "He'll bring my secret to the grave."

There, now it's all over. He will rest in peace, as they say, and she, too, will have peace.

The ceremony is brief. Ludovic's parents are staunch atheists and didn't want a service. Instead they have asked everyone to come back to their house after the burial for a memorial. Everyone prepared a poem, a story, a recording of a song Ludovic had loved, some photos.

This is when Louise understands that she will not have peace after all. Every remembrance of Ludovic makes her feel as though she is being crucified; she cries so much that her friends consider stopping the memorial. The outpouring of friendship, love, and care is accusatory rather than consoling. With every word she grows more and more distressed. She can think of only one thing: she hasn't told the truth, she has betrayed them. She couldn't hate herself more if she had killed Ludovic with her bare hands.

Alice and Pierre-Yves witness the liquefaction of their ward with concern, and decide by mutual agreement to remove her from the group.

"The parents and alpinists and all the rest of them will just have to get along without her. If she stays, she'll have to be rushed to the psychiatric hospital tomorrow," says Alice firmly. "We'll go have some tea at my house and talk about something else."

Alice's apartment in the nineteenth arrondissement is a jewel box. It's stylish, but not very big. Being a freelancer is tough. It's overflowing with mismatched, unusual objects— the beginning of a collection of owls in all sizes, rows of dolls dressed in traditional folk costumes, African masks, paintings, photos that have been taped or pinned up haphazardly. You can barely see the color of the wallpaper underneath the avalanche of shelves and furniture. But the apartment gives off the same air of vitality as its owner.

The bric-a-brac gives Alice the opportunity to start telling story after story about each object. Pierre-Yves starts to worry that it'll take a week for her to get through them all.

But one look at Louise's puffy face and he decides to begin recounting stories of his own: the trials and tribulations he faced during his early days at the paper; his coworkers' tics; the scandals of the famous Marion, the redhead in charge of the culture section.

The jasmine tea is perfect and the Ladurée macarons excellent. One would think it was simply a nice evening gathering of friends intended to hold the cranky winter evening, and especially the dug-up earth at the Antony cemetery, at a distance.

"I lied."

Louise drops this bombshell in a low voice, taking advantage of a pause in the conversation. A stunned silence follows. The other two try to pretend they hadn't heard anything.

"I lied, I lied to all of you. That's not how it actually happened."

Her voice is rising in pitch, like a child who wants to make sure the adults understand her.

Alice's hand freezes in midair, the mug of tea never reaching her mouth, and she winces. This tone never signals anything good. Pierre-Yves is the first to pull himself together. This is his job. He nearly takes out his graph-lined notebook.

"What are you saying, Louise? When did you lie? About what?"

Louise lowers her head. She cannot look at them. They had been her friends. But now they will hate her. She couldn't hold back anymore; she no longer has the strength. In this nice apartment with the two people who have been supporting her since she got back, she should be feeling more protected than ever. The Ludovic chapter of her life is over, and she's supposed to be free from torment. But it's precisely because the threat is over that she is forced to face the situation. If she alone is carrying this burden, she'll never manage to move on.

"The eye was in the tomb, watching Cain": she had stumbled through this line in school when they were reading the Victor Hugo poem.

The eye that's following her is the one that was looking out from the pile of rags, months ago already. It haunts her still. She can't forget its infinite weariness, the way it was both stunned and relieved to see her, but also indescribably sad. She couldn't have said whether it was the despondency of death or of treason that finished it off. Louise can no longer be alone with that stare.

She tells them everything. She doesn't try to explain what is inexplicable; she just talks, one word at a time, trying to re-create the sequence of the cold, hard facts.

Afterward there is a long silence. Maybe the other two are waiting for more revelations, or maybe they are simply thinking, watching the darkness invade the windows.

Alice is the one who breaks the stillness. She gets up and goes to sit next to Louise, putting her arm around Louise's shoulders, like she likes to do.

"Darling, that's what's torturing you? But you did the right thing."

She waits a few seconds to make sure that the words have sunk in.

"Yes, you absolutely did the right thing, the whole time. Everything you've said since the beginning about Ludovic lines up. There was a point when he let go and stopped fighting. That day he got sick, and his fate was sealed, whether you left or not. It's a terrible thing to say, but you had nothing to do with it."

She takes a deep breath before going on:

"I told you that one of my brothers committed suicide. He had been struggling for years, after some nasty harassment at work. He wasn't living anymore, he wasn't fighting. My other brother and my mother and I did everything we could. We took him on vacations, accompanied him to his treatments, introduced him to friends. I even stayed with him for weeks to distract him, talk to him, plead with him. It didn't do any good. You did what you had to do. You saved yourself."

Pierre-Yves suddenly realizes that this is it, the element he's been looking for ever since the beginning, the one that he had sensed. A primitive confrontation with life, one that forces you to act without regard to any code or rule, or even your own feelings. Louise's admission is the key piece of the book. Now her story has something universal to it.

Louise bursts into tears. She has curled up into fetal position on the couch. It's impossible to know if she has heard, never mind understood, Alice's soothing speech. She is sobbing so much she can barely breathe. She hiccups, grunts, chokes as though her throat isn't big enough to let out this outpouring of tension mixed with fear and disgust. The other two are stunned by the violence. Alice puts her hand on Lou-

ise's shoulder, murmuring "There . . . there . . ." ineffec-
tively.

Pierre-Yves says softly:

"Well, I think she has to sleep. Can you watch her tonight?
She can't possibly return to the hotel. Do you have sleeping
pills? Poor thing! To think that she's had that on her conscience the whole time."

Alice sleeps on the couch. Louise had allowed Alice to
undress her, going as limp as a rag doll, and then she fell
into a heavy sleep, thanks as much to the pills as to her nervous exhaustion. First thing tomorrow, Alice is going to telephone Valère, the psychologist she calls whenever her clients
have crises.

I T IS ALMOST ten a.m. Louise has just emerged, her face
swollen. She's taken two aspirins and drank just as many
coffees and is picking at a croissant. Pierre-Yves arrives with
flowers in hand. He's wearing the same houndstooth jacket
he had worn the first time they met, in London. This gives
Louise a start, bringing her back to reality. For a few minutes, they carefully discuss the color of Pierre-Yves's poin-
settias and the nasty weather that's turning the sky dark.
They're all dancing around the revelations of the previous
evening, afraid of setting off another crisis, but it's all they
can think about.

Finally, Alice begins:

"Louise, how are you feeling? I called one of my friends
this morning, Dr. Valère. He's a great guy, a psychologist.

He's ready to see you whenever you want. Or if you'd prefer, I also have a friend with a house in the Luberon who's agreed to let us stay there."

Louise sighs, which Alice interprets as a sign of acquiescence. So she continues:

"I'll say again what I said yesterday. You did the right thing. Anyone with any sense would have done what you did . . ."

She doesn't have time to elaborate. Pierre-Yves jumps in:

"The Luberon is an excellent idea. I'll go with you. It'll be nice and quiet for the three of us and we can start the book over again."

He had worked during part of the night and feels exhilarated in a way he rarely has before. He knows now that the first trip that Louise had taken to the scientific base is the climax—the crux, as alpinists say—of the story. He had looked at his notes again, this time recognizing that everything led to this part. Now he is ready to write about the lures and deterrents that had gone to war inside this woman's forsaken, helpless head. On one side love, humanity; on the other side, survival instinct.

"Stop bothering us with your book. Louise needs vacation and oblivion."

Pierre-Yves tries to be accommodating:

"Okay, no worries—we'll go on walks, we'll go to Lourmarin, to Gordes, to Bonnieux. I know some excellent restaurants, and at this time of year, we'll be left in complete peace. Don't worry, mother hen, I'm not going to overwhelm your chick with work. But we have to turn in a draft in a

month. We can't wait too long to publish and now that we
have to rethink everything, there's tons of work to do. I can
do most of it, but I'll still need Louise sometimes to explain
some things to me. And all three of us will need to figure
out how to handle the announcement."

"What announcement?"

"I mean when we're going to set the record straight. I
think it would be better to do it before the book comes out."

"Set the record straight?!" Alice gives him a furious look.
"Okay, Mr. Attorney General, where do you think you are?
In a courtroom? Louise told us something because she
trusted us, not because she wanted us to broadcast it from
the rooftops."

"Maybe, but now that we know, we can't pretend that we
don't. I'm going to need to talk about it in the book."

This seems so obvious to Pierre-Yves that he's caught off
guard by Alice's rage.

"We don't give a shit about your book!"

Alice has sat up straight on the couch as though she's pre-
paring to pounce on him. Louise, who has only ever seen
Alice smiling and relaxed, is bewildered to see her with blazing eyes and red cheeks.

"Don't tell me that you're planning to blab. What right do
you have? You know what's going to happen if you tell everyone? You'll stab Louise in the back! You know how media
people are. You're one of them, and I am, too. We live off
these things, spilled secrets."

"But it'll be leaked anyway at some point," protests Pierre-
Yves. "Louise told us yesterday. She might tell other people

later. So really it's on us to break the news in the right way. We have the upper hand now, we can take advantage of it."

"In the right way?! Are you fucking kidding me? You know perfectly well it will be the death knell for Louise. They'll destroy her with just as much intensity as they praised her. Even worse, because they'll feel like they fell for something. She won't have a moment's peace. They'll call on Ludovic's parents for backup and request an indictment for failing to assist a person in danger. Is that what you want? Louise, tell him!"

Louise is mute. She's folded herself up among the cushions, listening to them argue. Yesterday, she had felt relieved after admitting everything. This morning, another abyss is opening up in front of her. She's going to need to pay. Alice's rage hasn't reassured her. Are they really going to pursue her? It'll be the end of everyone's friendliness, indulgent TV presenters, people bending over backward to help her. She imagines magazine covers proclaiming her a "traitor," "liar," "mythomaniac," all accompanied by a hideous photo of her looking shifty. She realizes that she had underestimated the consequences. She's plagued by her vulnerability. No longer is she in control of her own fate; instead she is in the hands of these two people, allegedly her friends, who are already arguing. So she stays quiet, doggedly smoothing down the armrest.

Alice takes pity on the silent Louise and calms down a little. She no longer wants to fight with Pierre-Yves. She respects him. He's the one who gave her this job. She changes tactics.

"Listen, for a month now I've been giving you free publicity to set your book up, okay? I've gotten all the French and English channels, from *Télérama* to *Voici* and from France Culture to BFM. Louise is a heroine. Everyone knows her, everyone loves her—I wouldn't be surprised if she receives the Legion of Honor. She fought, she did crazy stuff. Neither you nor I could have done half the things she did, okay? And you want to ruin everything because there's one detail she didn't talk about, which doesn't even change the story? You know very well that all the people who were lazing around in front of their TVs while she was dying of hunger are going to feel entitled to judge her. And that would really suck, because they will never understand anything. Every wretched person on earth is going to share their opinion on Twitter or Facebook. It's so great to destroy someone you used to love!"

Alice forces herself to return to her usual light, professional tone of voice.

"She has a meeting next week to do a screen test with Miromont. If it goes well, she might get her first little role. I'm sure she'll be good. If you play your cards right, we might be able to get the guy there to adapt your book. Doesn't that sound good to you? But you know he won't do anything for a girl who's about to be labeled a quitter and a liar."

Pierre-Yves is thinking about things differently. "Quitter," "liar"—those are just words. What he's excited about is the confrontation with reality.

"Well," he says, in a falsely calm tone of voice, "we aren't on the same wavelength. I disagree. What Louise told us is incredibly powerful and it's going to make people even more interested in her story. I'm not at all sure that they're going to pile on her."

He pretends he's taking a second to choose his words carefully.

"You do publicity, I do journalism. I have a piece of information and it's my job to share it. Don't worry, I know how to put it in perspective, and I absolutely don't want to do any harm to Louise. You know that, right, Louise?" This time he's the one to appeal to her, without getting any more of a response.

"To be totally honest," he continues, "ever since the beginning I've suspected that there was something a little off about this story. I have a bit of a knack for these things." He's lowered his voice modestly. "So now we'll start over from the beginning. Louise, we'll keep working as a team, but please, don't hide anything else from me."

"A knack for these things! Putting it in perspective!" Alice explodes again. "You're just like all the others, a guy who's interested only in himself. Your so-called knack is for attacking a defenseless girl. You disgust me! And now you're insinuating that she's lied about other things? Hey, why not ask her if she discreetly killed the guy and sunk the boat herself, while you're at it?"

"I don't know about that. Only Louise knows."

"You asshole!"

Pierre-Yves jumps to his feet.

"Come on, let's stop it with the name-calling. I think we all need to calm down. Louise, I'll call you tomorrow. We'll talk about it calmly, and don't worry, there won't be any negative consequences for you."

He gathers up his coat quickly and slips away, leaving the two women on the couch dumbfounded. Alice pulls Louise toward her again.

"Poor darling, you didn't need all of that. That idiot doesn't understand anything. Like I told you, I've already been through things like this. I'm still haunted by the idea that I could have prevented my brother from going through with it. But every psychologist knows that you can't give someone the survival instinct if they don't already have it. You and I have it; they didn't. It's a terrible thing to say, but it's true. Listen, tomorrow you'll just need to tell that sleazy journalist that you made a mistake, or that you were so upset after the burial that you were just saying nonsense—that you were blaming yourself for not having been able to save Ludovic and you made it all up. He won't be able to prove anything anyway and it won't be in his interest to allude to anything because that would definitely lead to a libel suit. He won't risk it. And if I have to, I'll be your witness and you'll win. I strongly advise you to abandon this damn book, I'll help you cancel the contracts."

She lets out a big breath and pastes on a smile again.

"You have to promise me not to talk about this to anyone ever again. Or just to a psychologist, if that would help you. Like I told you, there's one waiting for you, and in that case you can count on patient confidentiality. Come on, promise me."

She takes Louise's chin in her hand and tips her face

upward, like you might do with a child when you're trying to make them promise something. But she is filled with anguish upon seeing Louise's empty stare; her pupils are pinpricks, absorbed by inner torment.

Alice knows this look. She saw it often, three years ago. It was the look in her brother's eyes.

LOUISE HAS DONE everything wrong, failed at everything, lost everything. Ludovic is dead, and she doesn't have a job or an apartment. Her two best friends have just argued because of her. Her future is in tatters. She's going to need to give up on the cinema. The whole world will rise up against her, and she'll end up in court. Alice's solution isn't really a solution, because what Louise said was the truth, the one that's been torturing her for months. She knows she won't keep it a secret any longer.

It's not yet noon when she returns to the hotel. She gets undressed and takes two sleeping pills, contemplating the bottle for a long time, then gets into bed and turns on the TV. It's a way for her to not think.

The next morning is stunning. A nice northern wind has chased away the clouds. Louise looks out the window for quite some time, without really knowing where she is or what time it is. And then everything comes back to her. She doesn't move; she's waiting, without knowing what she's waiting for.

Two birds pass by. She thinks they're geese, an unusual sight in the Parisian skies, in the middle of their mysterious migration dictated entirely by instinct. A light flickers in her mind. She will imitate them: she'll leave, or rather she'll flee, leaving behind her this hopeless entanglement and disappearing—this time for good.

With a feeling of urgency, she gets up without taking the time to shower. Leaving her clothes in the wardrobe, she collects only her computer and phone and goes downstairs to pay her bill.

In the street, she heads straight for the metro: Montrouge, Montparnasse, and then the Air France shuttle to Charles de Gaulle Airport, as though she were any normal traveler with an actual destination. At the airport she consults the giant board of flights leaving in the next four hours. She has always loved this, the feeling that the world is right there at your fingertips. Lima? She almost went there on vacation once, before her friend group decided the tickets were too expensive . . . Why not? Or Auckland, truly the end of the world—exactly what she needs! But both flights are full. She tries Vancouver and Tahiti next, without better results. Finally she falls back on Glasgow. Less drastic, but she's in a hurry and she has to leave. She remembers a trip she'd taken to Ben Nevis, the highest peak in Scotland, with the inseparable Phil, Benoît, and Sam. The moors had smelled wonderful, and from the summit they could see a magnificent jumble of islands. Now, at the beginning of winter, there won't be a living soul there.

In one last impulse, to appease her conscience she quickly sends the same message to her parents, Pierre-Yves, Alice, and her friends from Number 40:

I need a vacation. I'm leaving for a few weeks. I probably won't have internet or phone access. Don't worry, I'm fine. Love, Louise.

She hopes this is enough, but adds an extra text just for Alice:

I'm absolutely fine!

THERE'S NOTHING GLOOMIER than Glasgow in December. Only the Christmas decorations give a yellowish glow to the austere facades. She doesn't linger, stopping only to grab a bag and some clothes from the local Debenhams before inquiring about somewhere to stay—a hotel, a rental, anything, as long as it's very peaceful. At the visitors' center she is charming, telling them about the book she has to write, and her need for concentration and solitude.

"Ah, yes, of course," the employee answers. "There's the Isle of Mull, or the Isle of Skye, charming villages, accessible by ferry every day . . . Or Islay, where the whiskey's from . . . That might help with inspiration," he adds, quite seriously. "Farther away? More remote?"

He wonders how dark her novel must be to require such an environment.

"Maybe Jura—two hundred inhabitants and just one hotel, although I'll have to check if it's even open during the winter . . . Definitely no internet access, but you can use your cell phone, of course . . . The cliffs look out over the Atlantic, and the ocean current is the strongest in all of Europe. It makes the water churn, it's spectacular . . ." He's trying to sell it to her anyway.

"You'll need to take a ninety-minute train to Clachan,

then two ferries—one to Islay and then one to Feolin, the ferry terminal on Jura."

Perfect! Louise sets off on her adventure as though she's trying to lose someone tailing her: a bus to the station, the train, and two ferries. The more complicated the trip becomes, and the flatter and more deserted the landscape, the better she feels. By the time the last ferry docks at a shoddy concrete slip, she is already breathing more freely.

The owner of the hotel, Mr. Terence, whose ruddy face and stubby legs make him seem perfectly adapted to the strong local wind, comes to pick her up at Feolin in a 4x4 that, from the looks of it, has been around for a while. It's pouring rain and the gusts make the truck sway from side to side. The driver, unperturbed, provides her with commentary on the twists and turns of the island's only road, which is not great to begin with and nearly impossible to see through the foggy windshield, the curtain of rain, and the growing darkness.

The hotel room has faded wallpaper, a crocheted quilt, and a little Formica wood-laminate desk. Everything smells like the kind of damp that will never go away. Like many places in the north, it is hot inside. Louise opens her bag like a sailor returning to port.

She gives a quick last glance to the messages on her phone. Pierre-Yves must be annoyed. He's left tons of messages, as have her parents, whom he must have contacted to try to find out where she went. She turns off the device without reading any of them, puts it into the antique wardrobe along with her computer, and burrows into the bed. She hadn't planned to do this, but she's going to sleep until she's better.

It's what comes to her naturally, a way to finally let out the inhuman tension that's been with her ever since that long-ago day when she and Ludovic went to look for a dry lake in a remote island.

She tells her hosts the same story about being a writer in search of tranquility. She gets up around nine, gulps down some toast spread with homemade cranberry jam and a big plate of eggs, bacon, and beans covered in a bland tomato sauce, and returns to her room, pretending that inspiration has struck. The bed calls to her and she curls back up in it, taking a sensual pleasure in pulling the duvet up to her chin and letting out voluntarily loud sighs. Even after a good night's sleep, she falls back asleep deeply, as though she is still haunted by dogged exhaustion. It has the same healing effect as during a bout of flu. While she's asleep, it seems to her that mysterious and beneficial connections are getting to work, repairing the wound she feels in her soul.

She reappears around one p.m., feigning having worked hard, and eats a plate of cold meat with mayonnaise. Then, no matter what the weather is like, she dons the parka she bought in Glasgow and goes outside for three hours straight. She's no longer scared of the cold or wind. They can rage as much as they want, toss her around, leave her drenched and dizzy. When she's had enough, the Terences will be there with the tea and scones that Mrs. Terence makes so well. She'll go back to her warm room, her bed, her den, and take a nap until dinner if that's what she feels like. She's no longer scared of anything.

For the first two weeks, she chooses which part of the coast to go to—facing the wind, or protected from it—depending on whether the weather is nice or gloomy and on whether she's feeling aggressive or peaceful. The little skeleton trees and dry grass seem to her like they match her state of mind. She, too, is waiting for springtime.

She walks quickly, letting her pants get wet from the ferns and gorse along the path. Regularly she stops to observe a motionless cormorant dry its wings as though it has all the time in the world, or a fishing boat fighting in the foam. The air makes her light-headed and relaxed, and it unravels the knots that have been deep down inside her, silent. Now she can replay even the most morbid images in her head; in her present state she no longer fears them. She can shout into the wind without risking anyone hearing her and misusing her words.

As she walks, the physical mechanism seems to set in motion the mental one. In this simple land of moors and gusts of wind, Louise can feel again what she often used to feel when climbing: that her body and mind are one. Every step and every breath she manages to take despite the mud and the wind stimulate her thoughts imperceptibly. Her mind grows more limber, and it makes her think of those ancient tools that she and Ludovic had painstakingly repaired in order to fix up the whaling ship. She can't think freely like this when she's immobile inside a bedroom. Her neurons are firing to the rhythm of her muscles.

It's an infinite relief to not have to fight her thoughts any longer. She returns to the hotel sated, her eyes red from the wind and her heart a little more peaceful each time.

One day it is sunny, and she takes advantage of it by going to the other side of the island. Mr. Terence obligingly drives her the thirty-five kilometers north from the village of Craighouse to the famous Corryvreckan, a narrow strait between the islands of Jura and Scarba.

"Continue along the path for around forty-five minutes and you'll find the old Barnhill farm, and then you'll cross the moors in the north. Be careful with the wind—it can easily throw you over the edge of the cliffs. I have some things to do, so I'll come get you around four p.m."

One side of Corryvreckan faces the waves of the Atlantic, while the other side serves as an emptying basin for the coastal lakes, meaning that the strait is constantly pummeled by furious currents of up to nine knots. To complicate matters further, a small island right in the middle renders the strait even narrower and more aggressive. Even on a calm day, it looks like giant boiling pots of water. The guy at the visitors' center hadn't lied.

Today, a sustained westerly wind battles tirelessly with the current going in the opposite direction. The sea panics, not knowing which master to obey. Waves break in all directions, spurting like geysers, bouncing off the lone rock, submerging their thirty meters as though they're playing leapfrog. The churning ocean changes from gray to a translucent green, sweeping along with it massive waves of yellowish foam. When the sun breaks through the clouds, it creates dozens of rainbows in the sea spray. Overall the impression is one of a primordial ferocity, raw power harassed by a group of demons. Even more terrifying are the sounds: the furious rumbling, the hissing, the growling of the water foaming with anger, as though it were about to miss an important meeting.

Louise is almost meditative as she faces all this noise. Nature again, always the strongest, just like on Stromness. In the countercurrents along the cliff, she sees clumps of branches and leaves forming tiny islands that are quickly broken up by the water's movements, which send them off dancing in all different directions. As soon as it seems like they will reach the shore, a wave catches them and herds them back into battle.

To Louise, this is almost an allegory of the last several months. She was a little twig, tossed around by her circumstances, incapable of ever getting to dry land. What she dreams of is calm waters, a peaceful current that will carry her along with it, gently and predictably, every day. And suddenly she bursts out laughing about the banality of this metaphor. She's laughing at herself, without any ulterior motive—something that hasn't happened since the first night she spent at the Hilton. That was so long ago. And yet it wasn't exactly the same kind of laugh. That one had been nervous, tense, uncomfortable, while today's is more free, more relieved. Because now she's no longer in the midst of the battle. She's safely on the shore and merely watching.

SHE'S NO LONGER sleeping fifteen hours a day. To fill the extra time, she borrows tattered paperbacks from the hotel's library: *Jane Eyre*, *The Mysterious Island*, anything she can find among the limited selection. She also tries her hand at sketching, which was something she'd been interested in as a teenager, and roams the moors with an old notebook that Mr. Terence found for her in his storeroom. Here you have to live on what you have already, or what you can improvise, while you're waiting for the boat to bring whatever you've ordered from Islay and from the rest of Europe.

The deprivation contributes to her salvation. No need to go to a lot of trouble; you just have to take what comes to you, fall into a daily routine.

She begins to chat more and more with Mrs. Terence, who likes to soothe her arthritis by sitting in the corner with the electric radiator that glows red like a fake fireplace. The good woman is very proud that George Orwell came here to write *1984*. Before he moved into Barnhill, he had spent a few weeks at the hotel, which at the time was owned by Mrs. Terence's mother and stepfather. Mrs. Terence remembers the tall, thin, somber man with the sad eyes. He never smiled, not even at her, a little girl. It's not surprising that he wrote such a dark book, one that gave her nightmares once she was old enough to read it.

"That poor widower," her mother used to say. "He's inconsolable!"

Louise feels a sense of empathy for the wounded being who, like her, had come here in search of some kind of peace.

Mrs. Terence has clearly formed a hypothesis about Louise, which she hints at with her line of questioning:

"Any kids . . . ? Will you go back to your family for Christmas?"

She is sure that the young woman is nursing heartbreak.

It's true, Christmas is coming. Louise spends it at the hotel, where she is the only guest. This earns her the privilege of partaking in the roast wild goose, which is delicious, and the pudding, which is less so. Between Christmas and New Year's, it snows a lot. She continues her walks with large boots, again provided by Mr. Terence.

"They belong to my daughter-in-law. I have to admit that the kids never come here in the winter anymore. They prefer the Balearic Islands!"

The only signs of life in the village occur around five p.m., when several employees from the distillery, which is across from the hotel, blow off work and come over to have a drink. It's always a bunch of unmarried men, and on Fridays, two older supervisors and an accountant join in. Louise envies their simple, almost monotonous conviviality. One beer, and then a second; comments about their work that day, a few stories about the village, complaints about Londoners, and vows to vote for Scottish independence, all in an accent so thick it swallows up half the words. Since this is often the time when she's returning from her walk, Louise is sometimes invited to join in.

"The book going well?" they ask her. "The next time it's nice out, you should go over to Cape Fenearah, you can see deer there . . ."

No one asks her anything else. She is part of the scenery now, just "the French writer." They don't want to know where she comes from, or what her life has been like, or what she's writing about.

One of the boys, Ed, has been eyeing her with interest. He tries his luck one day, suggesting that they go for a motorcycle ride on Saturday to the Islay distilleries. But Louise isn't ready yet for any kind of relationship, even a superficial one. Although she is beginning to recover in that area, too. The other night, before falling asleep, she had touched her breasts with one hand as the other gently worked its way down between her thighs, until finally, timidly, she made herself come. It was purely physical, but reassuring all the same: she was returning to some kind of normality.

One evening, Louise unearths *1984* and climbs into bed with it. She remembered parts of it. The scene with the rat torture, which had made a strong impression on her even the first time she'd read it, is particularly horrifying to her now that she herself has experienced how rapacious the animals are. But there is one thing that strikes her like a lightning bolt, and she rereads it three times. The hero of the novel, Winston, gets ahold of a book written by a man named Emmanuel Goldstein, supposedly the leader of the organization rebelling against Big Brother. In the book, the dissident unveils the methods of totalitarianism, and in the chapter on information there is one sentence that makes Louise's blood run cold: "Who controls the past controls the future. Who controls the present controls the past."

She's never felt like fiction was addressing her directly before, or thought that it could help her see things more clearly. Novels were stories. But now she realizes that they have a lot to do with real life.

Orwell was developing his argument. His society depends

on the infallibility of Big Brother. In order to stave off historical analysis, comparisons, and questioning, it was absolutely necessary to change the past to suit the present. Under Stalin's rule, they had retouched old photos of the Politburo to get rid of anyone who had ended up in the Gulag. The members of the Party must therefore believe in perpetuity that black is white and vice versa—what Orwell calls "doublethink."

That was exactly what Louise herself had nearly done: misrepresent her past. Rewriting her story hadn't been without advantages, but it had made her guilt worse. Like Orwell, she had fled. Putting this harm into words is a relief for her, the climax of the maturation she feels she has been undergoing ever since she got to Jura. She has been carrying two truths within her, and it's one too many. It's so simple when you look at it that way.

She gets up and opens the window, letting a puff of glacial air into the room. After a day of rain, the moonlit sky has regained a crystalline purity. Every grove, every tree, every branch stands out against the snowy background with a surrealist clarity. That is what she wants: purity, truth.

She'll bring herself with her; never again will she let herself write off her own past, like the citizens of Oceania. Never will she say that she doesn't know what two and two make, like Orwell's poor Winston. This vow makes her feel like a resistance fighter.

Will she ever untangle the reasons for her actions on Stromness? What's the point of going over and over what was just an impulse? Introspection won't change anything;

it will just leave her mired in remorse. As a child, she had dreamed of being a heroine. But life makes a mockery of dreams. Her time in the darkness has caused her to grow up. She's no longer "the little one."

Louise starts to shiver in the breeze. But she stays where she is, as though she wants her body to remember this remarkable moment as much as her mind will. It's the middle of the night, but she considers going on a pilgrimage to the house with the blue shutters where it seems like a man had held out his hand to her, seventy years earlier.

She inhales deeply, and the freezing wind burns her windpipe. She imagines that it's scouring her clean from the inside out.

THE NEXT DAY, it snows heavily. As soon as it calms down, Louise sets out on a five-hour struggle to reach Beinn an Òir, which at 785 meters is the highest peak on the island.

At first she follows the edge of the forest, where the snow is less dense. But quickly she reaches the prairie and can no longer see the footpath. The steeper the incline, the harder it is for her to force her way onward. But she is stubborn, planting her fists in the thick carpet of snow for support, lifting her knees up to her chin, pushing forward with even her stomach. Snow fills her boots and gets all the way up her sleeves. The blood pounding in her temples makes her dizzy. It doesn't bother her. The struggle is entertaining. The more tired she becomes, the more it seems as though a vital life force is finally coming back to her. This vigor is her personal brand, what has always allowed her to keep going—to believe in herself when she was ignored as a teenager, to find her way through life, to survive when all seemed lost. Her wanderings of the last few months had blocked this particular strength, but now she is rediscovering it with an inexpressible happiness. Alice was right: she can't do anything about it. This is how she is.

The previous night she had settled an old score. Now life is beginning again. She will always harbor pain, sadness, a death. She will bear a scar in Ludovic's name. Above all she doesn't want to forget anymore.

As she makes her way up the mountain, she savors the view that is beginning to unveil itself. Finally she gets to the last bit of incline, and the island stretches out at her feet. From up here, the view is astonishing, bringing with it a feeling of power. On one side are islands as far as the eye can see, riddled with fjords, and the purplish-blue foothills of the old Caledonian massif; on the other side is the North Atlantic, a greenish gray flecked with white from the constantly breaking waves.

Louise understands that she no longer needs the modest refuge of Jura. She is even eager to leave, like a patient who's fed up with staying in bed. She is going to return to the front lines, find a job, friends, lovers.

Crouched on top of the mountain, in front of the islands that are beginning to be bathed in pink and gray, Louise stares straight ahead. Sweat is running down her back. Automatically she is windmilling her arms to warm herself up again. She needs to start her descent. It will be the last walk she'll take on the island.

Her future won't be shaped around a film or a book. The media cycle turns quickly. In a few months, no one will recognize her anymore; in a few years, her adventure will be completely forgotten.

And in the meantime? Should she melt into the Scottish mist? Her degree must mean something; she speaks English fluently. Surely, between oil, tourism, and mining, they need accountants. She's ready to do anything: she could translate or be a tour guide in Glasgow, Oban, Aberdeen. The feeling that a blank slate awaits her is both thrilling and dizzying.

It's not yet four p.m., and the light is fading quickly. Ignoring the path she had made on her way up, Louise hurtles down the pure snow slope in ecstasy.

Exactly one year ago, the *Jason* had entered the Beagle Channel, bringing two kids intoxicated with happiness to an island full of promise.